the written

BY BEN GALLEY

ART BY MIKE SHIPLEY

IT WAS SNOWING OUTSIDE. THE WHITE FLAKES FELL LAZILY IN THE NIGHT BREEZE, DUSTING THE ROCKY MOUNTAINSIDE WITH AN IVORY BLANKET.
A TALL SPIRE ROSE FROM AN OUTCROP OF QUIET BUILDINGS AMONGST THE SNOWY CRAGS, WHERE ONE LONELY YELLOW WINDOW GLOWED BRIGHTLY THROUGH THE BLIZZARD.
FRAMED BY THE LIGHT, A VERY OLD MAN STOOD AT THE WINDOWSILL WITH HIS ARMS CROSSED. HE SIGHED WITH TIREDNESS AND FOUGHT BACK YET ANOTHER YAWN.
BEHIND HIM, GATHERED AROUND A DESK AND PORING OVER A SMALL SQUARE BOOK, SAT A GROUP OF FOUR EQUALLY AGED MEN. THE ROOM WAS CAVERNOUS AND PACKED FLOOR TO CEILING WITH BURSTING BOOKSHELVES, EACH ONE FILLED WITH AN IMPOSSIBLE AMOUNT OF PAPER AND KNOWLEDGE.
I DON'T EVEN THINK IT'S SIREN.
OF COURSE IT IS, INNEL, JUST LOOK AT THE SCALES OF THE FRONT COVER!
NO, NO NOT AS YET. THEY'RE ALWAYS LATE...
FIFTEEN YEARS LATER AND ONLY NOW DO WE GET TO STUDY THIS MANUSCRIPT. WHO KNOWS THE INCALCULABLE VALUE OF THE MAGICK HELD INSIDE THIS BOOK, SO THE QUESTION REMAINS, HOW DO WE GET THE CONFOUNDED THING OPEN? HAVE WE HAD A REPLY FROM KRAUSLUNG YET, GERNN?
THE MAN TRIED ONCE AGAIN TO SPLIT A FEW PAGES APART WITH A LONG YELLOW FINGERNAIL, BUT THE BOOK WAS LOCKED FAST, AND NOT EVEN THE TIP OF A KNIFE BLADE COULD SQUEEZE BETWEEN THEM.

TWGNPB1:
ISBN: 978-0-9927871-3-4
FIRST EDITION
PUBLISHED BY BENGALLEY.COM
COVER DESIGN BY MIKE SHIPLEY
STORY BY BEN GALLEY
ART BY MIKE SHIPLEY

WANT A PHYSICAL VERSION AS WELL? NOT A PROBLEM. THIS
GRAPHIC NOVEL IS ALSO AVAILABLE IN PAPERBACK FROM
ALL MAJOR BOOKSHOPS AND ONLINE STORES.

JUST HEAD TO WWW.BENGALLEY.COM TO FIND OUT MORE.

THE WRITTEN GRAPHIC NOVEL WAS
FUNDED BY KICKSTARTER AND 166
AMAZING BACKERS, RAISING OVER £5,500
TO BRING THIS PROJECT TO LIFE.

KICKSTARTER

FIND OUT MORE ABOUT THEM AT THE END
OF THE NOVEL.

WELL NOTHING'S CHANGED SINCE THIS AFTERNOON. THE BLOODY THING'S STILL LOCKED TIGHTER THAN A VAMPYRE'S COFFIN. NONE OF US HERE POSSESS THE SKILL TO UNLOCK IT.
I SUGGEST WE JUST WAIT FOR...
GERNN WAS INTERRUPTED BY THE SOUNDS OF HEAVY BOOTS ON STONE.
THE SCHOLARS WERE A LITTLE STARTLED TO SAY THE LEAST.
HAVING TROUBLE, WISE MEN OF ARFELL?
A TALL HOODED MAN EMERGED FROM THE DOORWAY, HANDS CLASPED BEHIND HIS BACK AND A WARM SMILE ON HIS FACE.
AS HE MOVED FROM THE SHADOWS AND INTO THE CANDLELIGHT, THEY QUICKLY RECOGNISED A FAMILIAR FACE. THE MAN THREW BACK HIS HOOD. A CHORUS OF RESPECTFUL SMILES FOLLOWED.
YOUR MAGE, WHAT AN UNEXPECTED HONOUR! WHAT, WITH THE WEATHER AND ALL WE DIDN'T EXPECT YOU OR ADDREN TO ARRIVE FOR ANOTHER TWO DAYS
DON'T BE RIDICULOUS. THE WEATHER HAS NEVER STOPPED ME. WHEN WE HEARD THAT YOU HAD UNCOVERED A LONG LOST BOOK OF SECRETS, I DECIDED THAT NO TIME SHOULD BE WASTED IN COMING TO SEE IT.
IT IS MOST DEFINITELY SIREN, SIRE, AS WE THOUGHT.
BUT THIS BOOK IS NOT FROM RECENT YEARS, YOUR MAGE. IT'S ANCIENT. BUT AS YET, WE HAVEN'T BEEN ABLE TO OPEN IT. THERE IS A STRONG LOCK SPELL ON THE COVER, AND NO KEY FOR ITS LATCH.
IF IT IS LEGIBLE, THEN WE CAN READ IT, YOUR MAGE. WE MEN OF ARFELL HAVE STUDIED EVERY TONGUE KNOWN IN EMANESKA. THERE ISN'T A BOOK IN THESE LANDS WE COULDN'T TRANSLATE.

PERHAPS I COULD HELP. . .
THE TALL MAN MUTTERED AN INCANTATION UNDER HIS BREATH AS HE REACHED TOWARDS THE BOOK, HIS FINGERS RIGID AND OUTSPREAD. A TINY RIPPLE OF AIR PULSATED FROM HIS HAND LIKE A WAVE OF HEAT OVER A FIRE.
THIS BOOK IS STRONG.
CLICK
AS THE BOOK RATTLED ON THE DESK, THE SCHOLARS SWAPPED MIXED LOOKS OF EXCITEMENT AND UNCERTAINTY.
BLUE SPARKS BEGAN TO DANCE OVER ITS COVER, BUT AS ABRUPTLY AS THEY HAD APPEARED, THEY VANISHED, AND THE THICK METAL LATCH POPPED OPEN WITH A LOUD CLICK.
BLINKING HIS MISTY EYES, THE OLDEST SCHOLAR LIFTED THE LATCH AND TURNED THE ANCIENT COVER WITH CAREFUL FINGERS. IT CREAKED AS HE LOWERED IT REVERENTLY TO THE DESK.
READ YOUR BOOK, GENTLEMEN.
...'SUMMONING'.
IT'S ELVISH, DARK ELF, IF I'M NOT MISTAKEN. I... I HAVEN'T SEEN A TEXT LIKE THIS FOR YEARS, IT READS...
THE TESTAMENT OF BRINGING BUT THAT WORD COULD ALSO MEAN, ERM CREATING, OR...
SUMMONING?
AS I'M SURE YOU KNOW, SIRE, THE DARK ELVES WERE POWERFUL CREATURES, CAPABLE OF CONTROLLING THE DARKEST OF ALL MAGICKS.

THEIR ACOLYTES COULD SUMMON HUGE BEASTS FROM THE DARKEST PLACES OF THE WORLD AT THE CAST OF A SINGLE SPELL.
GERNN WENT TO A BOOKSHELF AND BROUGHT BACK A RARE SCRAP OF TAPESTRY COVERED WITH CRUDE PICTURES DEPICTING BATTLES WITH STRANGE GOBLIN-TYPE ANIMALS AND GIANT WINGED CREATURES WITH MANY HORNS WEARING WHAT LOOKED TO BE GOLDEN CROWNS.
WHERE ARE THE KEYS?
I DON'T DARE TO READ ALOUD ANY FURTHER; IT SEEMS WE HAVE UNCOVERED A VERY SPECIAL BOOK INDEED.
FOR THIS SPELL? ERM, THERE, AND THE OTHER, THERE. THESE ARE THE MAIN WORDS, ME AND HEAR, SAYING THEM IN THE OTHER ORDER, OF COURSE, WOULD BEGIN THE SPELL.
IT SEEMS TO REFERENCE SOMETHING CALLED 'THY DARKNESS SWALLOWED,' OR ... 'MOUTHS OF DARKNESS.'
HOW INTERESTING THIS ALL IS.
HAHA, AND WITHOUT YOU, OLD FOOLS.
WELL, IT SEEMS YOU HAVE BEEN MOST USEFUL TO ME THIS EVENING. I AM SURE ADDREN WILL BE AS PLEASED AS I AM TO HEAR ABOUT THIS.
THANK YOU, SIRE. WE WILL CONTINUE TO STUDY THIS MANUAL WITH DILIGENCE, THERE IS MUCH MORE KNOWLEDGE TO BE GAINED FROM IT, WITHOUT YOU, MY LORD, WE WOULD PROBABLY STILL HAVE A LOCKED BOOK.
I WOULD HAVE NOTHING!

WITH A BURST OF IMMENSE SPEED, THE MAGE DREW HIS SWORD IN A SILVER BLUR AND SLAMMED THE BLADE INTO INNEL'S CHEST.
THE MAGE THEN SWUNG HIS BLADE TO THE RIGHT AND CUT THE THROAT OF THE OLD SCHOLAR. DARK BLOOD PAINTED THE BOOKSHELVES.
SPARKS OF ELECTRICITY DANCED AROUND THE MAGE'S FINGERS. A HUGE BOLT OF LIGHTNING ENVELOPED THE OTHER SCHOLARS, BURNING THEM TO A CRISP IN A MATTER OF SECONDS. AN ACRID SMOKE FILLED THE ROOM.
HIS BUSINESS CONCLUDED, THE MAGE CALMLY SHEATHED HIS SWORD AND TOOK THE BLACK BOOK FROM THE DESK.
WIPING THE BLOOD FROM ITS COVER, HE TURNED ON HIS HEEL, PICKED UP HIS ROBES FROM THE CHAIR, AND LEFT WITHOUT ANOTHER SOUND.

FAR TO THE WEST, IN NORTHERN ALBION, A HOODED STRANGER WAS MARCHING THROUGH THE WILDERNESS. HE HAD TRAVELLED WITHOUT REST FOR TWO DAYS, HEADING SOUTH THROUGH FIELD AND FOREST AND RIVER AND HILL.
THE MAN WAS TREADING THROUGH THE THICK LOAM OF THE FOREST OF DURN, A SHADY WOOD SOUTH OF LEATH THAT WAS SELDOM ENTERED OR EXPLORED BY THE ITS TOWNSPEOPLE.
RUMOUR HAD IT A VAMPYRE LIVED IN THE DARK, DAMP WOODS. FEW LOCAL SOULS HAD THE GALL TO PROVE THE RUMOURS WRONG. THOSE THAT DID WERE NEVER SEEN AGAIN. THE STRANGER SEEMED COMPLETELY UNPERTURBED BY SUCH RUMOURS.
THE THICK, GNARLED TREES GAVE WAY TO REVEAL A SMALL GLADE AND A TALL BRICK BUILDING THAT HAD BEEN COMPLETELY CONCEALED BY THE FOREST. THIS WAS AN ARKABBEY, ONE OF MANY THAT COULD BE FOUND DOTTED THROUGHOUT THE WILDS OF ALBION AND EMANESKA, KEEPING WATCH ON THE WILDERNESS.

THE MAN STRODE INSIDE THE ARCH AND FELT THE WARMTH OF THE BUSY BUILDING ON HIS COLD SKIN.
THE MAN OPENED THE DOOR TO HIS ROOM WITH A BANG, STARTLING THE MAID WITHIN.
OH! FARDEN, IT'S YOU.
SAME OLD.
YOU COULD HAVE KNOCKED.
TO MY OWN ROOM? YOU SHOULDN'T BE SNEAKING AROUND IN HERE.
ELESSI WAS HIS MAID AND FRIEND OF MANY YEARS. SHE WAS A SIMPLE SOUL, TOO CURIOUS FOR HER OWN GOOD, BUT SHE HAD ALWAYS LOOKED AFTER HIM WELL.
GODS KNOW SOMEONE NEEDS TO LOOK AFTER YOU MAGICK LOT. DURNUS IS WAITING FOR YOU UPSTAIRS.
A THIN OLD MAN SAT WITH HIS BACK TO THE DOOR, WATCHING THE FLAMES CRACKLE AND POP IN THE FIREPLACE. DRAPES HUNG THICK AND HEAVY OVER THE WINDOWS, MAKING THE HUGE ROOM DIM AND FULL OF FLICKERING SHADOWS. CANDLES DOTTED THE FLOORS AND WALLS, ENSCONCED IN HOLDERS AND PERCHING ON TALL PILES OF BOOKS.

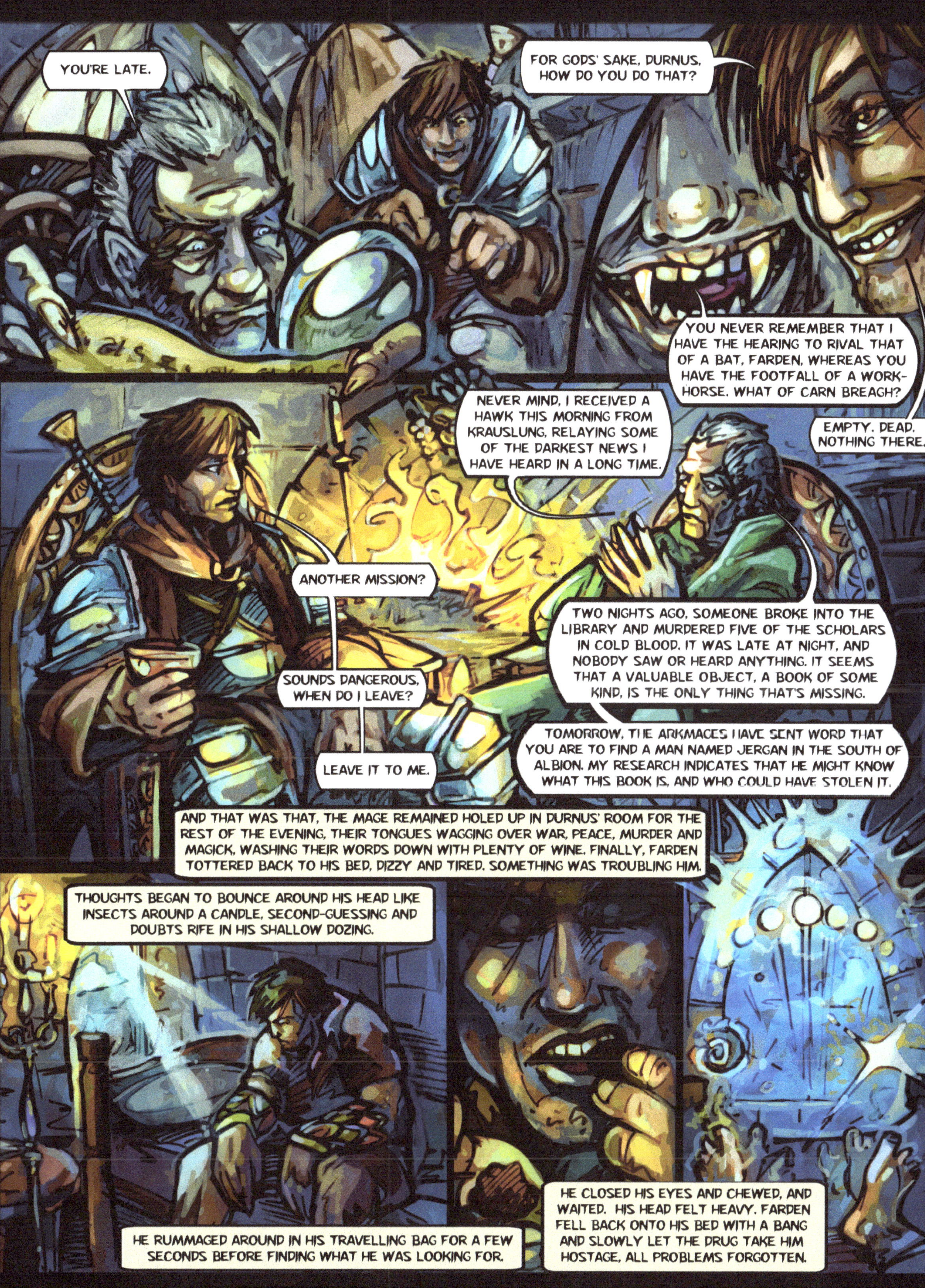

YOU'RE LATE.
FOR GODS' SAKE, DURNUS, HOW DO YOU DO THAT?
YOU NEVER REMEMBER THAT I HAVE THE HEARING TO RIVAL THAT OF A BAT, FARDEN, WHEREAS YOU HAVE THE FOOTFALL OF A WORK-HORSE. WHAT OF CARN BREACH?
EMPTY. DEAD. NOTHING THERE.
NEVER MIND, I RECEIVED A HAWK THIS MORNING FROM KRAUSLUNG, RELAYING SOME OF THE DARKEST NEWS I HAVE HEARD IN A LONG TIME.
ANOTHER MISSION?
TWO NIGHTS AGO, SOMEONE BROKE INTO THE LIBRARY AND MURDERED FIVE OF THE SCHOLARS IN COLD BLOOD. IT WAS LATE AT NIGHT, AND NOBODY SAW OR HEARD ANYTHING. IT SEEMS THAT A VALUABLE OBJECT, A BOOK OF SOME KIND, IS THE ONLY THING THAT'S MISSING.
SOUNDS DANGEROUS, WHEN DO I LEAVE?
TOMORROW, THE ARKMAGES HAVE SENT WORD THAT YOU ARE TO FIND A MAN NAMED JERGAN IN THE SOUTH OF ALBION. MY RESEARCH INDICATES THAT HE MIGHT KNOW WHAT THIS BOOK IS, AND WHO COULD HAVE STOLEN IT.
LEAVE IT TO ME.
AND THAT WAS THAT, THE MAGE REMAINED HOLED UP IN DURNUS' ROOM FOR THE REST OF THE EVENING, THEIR TONGUES WAGGING OVER WAR, PEACE, MURDER AND MAGICK, WASHING THEIR WORDS DOWN WITH PLENTY OF WINE. FINALLY, FARDEN TOTTERED BACK TO HIS BED, DIZZY AND TIRED. SOMETHING WAS TROUBLING HIM.
THOUGHTS BEGAN TO BOUNCE AROUND HIS HEAD LIKE INSECTS AROUND A CANDLE, SECOND-GUESSING AND DOUBTS RIFE IN HIS SHALLOW DOZING.
HE RUMMAGED AROUND IN HIS TRAVELLING BAG FOR A FEW SECONDS BEFORE FINDING WHAT HE WAS LOOKING FOR.
HE CLOSED HIS EYES AND CHEWED, AND WAITED. HIS HEAD FELT HEAVY. FARDEN FELL BACK ONTO HIS BED WITH A BANG AND SLOWLY LET THE DRUG TAKE HIM HOSTAGE, ALL PROBLEMS FORGOTTEN.

THE MAGE WAS IN A DESERT. IT WAS HOT. HE WAS DIZZY, AND DREAMING. DEFINITELY DREAMING. HE FELT SOMETHING SCRATCHING AT HIS LEG AND LOOKED DOWN TO FIND A SKINNY BLACK CAT IMPATIENTLY CLAWING AT HIM. CONFUSED, HE LIFTED HIS HANDS TO HIS FACE AND FELT THE CHARRED BONE UNDERNEATH, AND WATCHED SHREDS OF FLAMING SKIN FILL THE AIR LIKE A SWARM OF LOCUSTS IN THE SUDDEN HOT WIND. THE MAGE HEARD A VOICE IN HIS HEAD SPEAK CLEARLY OVER THE FIRE AND THE ROARING WIND.

THE FOLLOWING MORNING, A GROGGY FARDEN MET DURNUS IN THE MAIN HALL. FARDEN BOWED HIS HEAD AND BRIEFLY KNELT BEFORE AN EFFIGY OF EVERNIA, THE ARKA'S GODDESS OF MAGICK.

AFTER DURNUS HAD GIVEN FARDEN A MAP AND BID HIM GOOD FORTUNE, THE MAGE JOGGED OVER THE WET ARKABBEY LAWN AND INTO THE THICK FOREST. HE DISAPPEARED BEHIND THE TREES, AND DURNUS RETURNED TO HIS ROOM, SAYING MORE THAN A FEW CHARMS FOR LUCK.

let it be not said that Farden is just simply skilled;
the man is far and above any mage I have yet to encounter.
Dispite their downfalls, he is part of a powerful family, a pure breed.
Whatever the scribe wrote into his Book awoke a magick beast inside him.
I've never seen a mage withstand such draining as he does,
nor weild such spells with ease. It's a shame he ruins it all with his anger,
his battle rage if you will, the red mist that has gotten him into trouble
and danger many times before. Just look at what happened in Husker
after he killed the chieftan's son in that fist fight, all for some rediculous wager.

If Farden learnt to turn his anger into concentration, he would be
greater than the Arkmages, and if that's treason you can hang me for it.

TAKEN FROM THE DIARY OF DURNUS GLASSREN.

IT WAS RAINING HARD WHEN FARDEN WALKED THROUGH THE INDUSTRIOUS STREETS OF BEINNH.
FARDEN TRUDGED THROUGH THE MUDDY PUDDLES AND CART RUTS, DODGING THE BROWN RIVERS OF RUBBISH.
THE MAGE SPOTTED A SMALL BLACKSMITH'S SHOP NESTLED IN THE BACK OF THE MARKETPLACE.
SEE SOMETHING YOU LIKE, BOY?
HOW MUCH FOR THIS, OLD MAN?
HMM. . .ONE 'UNDRED SILVER
ONE HUNDRED? YOU'VE GOT TO BE JOKING.
I'LL GIVE YOU SIXTY, FAIR PRICE FOR THIS BLADE.
EIGHTY, OR NO SALE.
Blacksmith

SIXTY, AND YOU CAN HAVE THAT, OLD MAN, IT'S STILL GOT A FEW SWINGS IN IT.
FARDEN NOTICED THE SILENCE AT THE TABLE. A GROUP OF STOCKY MEN WERE HUNCHED OVER WATCHING THE TRANSACTION.
FARDEN TURNED TO MEET THE STARE OF A BALD THUG WITH A SCAR ACROSS HIS FOREHEAD.
THE MAN HELD THE MAGE'S PIERCING GAZE A MOMENT BEFORE TURNING AWAY TO GRIN AT HIS MATES.
YE WANT THAT TOO?
HEY SMITH, IS THAT MIRROR SILVER?
THE GRIM MAN LEFT, HIS MINIONS FOLLOWING HIM LIKE LOYAL DOGS.
THIS IS IMPORTANT OLD MAN, THIS MIRROR HAS TO BE PURE SILVER, YOU UNDERSTAND?
EASY, EASY, IT'S SILVER MATE
THE MAGE STEPPED BACK INTO THE POURING RAIN AND HEADED DOWN THE HILL TOWARDS THE SOUTH GATE OF THE MUDDY TOWN.

FARDEN WATCHED HIS OWN BOOTS TREAD THROUGH THE MUD, SENDING LITTLE BROWN RIVERS FLYING THROUGH THE AIR WITH EVERY STEP.
JUS' GIVE US YER SILVER AND WE'LL BE ON OUR WAY.
IF YOU AND YOUR MEN KNOW WHAT'S BEST FOR YOU THEN YOU'D BE ON YOUR WAY NOW.
LET'S NOT 'AVE ANY TROUBLE 'ERE, MATE.
GET 'IM LADS, GET 'IS COINS!
CRUNCH
THUDD
I'LL KILL YER!
TOOF'
DURNIUS WOULD NOT BE HAPPY WITH SUCH A VICIOUS DISPLAY . . . BUT DURNUS WASN'T THERE.

EIGHT HOURS LATER, A LONE FIGURE CROUCHED ON THE SUMMIT OF A LOW HILL, HIS LONG CLOAK BILLOWING IN THE STORMY WIND, RAIN LASHING HIS UNBLINKING FEATURES.
THE MAN WAS STARING AVIDLY AT A SMALL CANDLE-LIT HOVEL COWERING IN A SHALLOW VALLEY BETWEEN TWO HILLS.
HE SLOWLY CROUCHED DOWN AGAIN WITH SWORD IN HAND AND LOOKED BACK AT THE HUT.
THE CANDLE HAD GONE OUT...
SUDDENLY IN THE CORNER OF HIS EYE, SOMETHING SEEMED TO MOVE ON THE HILLSIDE.
FROM ABSOLUTELY NOWHERE, A MASSIVE SHAPE BOWLED OUT OF THE RAIN AND BARRELLED INTO THE MAGE, DRIVING THE AIR FROM HIS LUNGS.. HE FLEW DOWN THE HILL.
A SEARING LIGHT CUT THROUGH THE DARKNESS OF THE STORMY NIGHT, REVEALING A HULKING CREATURE STANDING A DOZEN YARDS DOWN THE HILLSIDE, MATTED HAIR DRENCHED WITH RAIN AND PLUMES OF HOT BREATH ESCAPING FROM A MOUTHFUL OF FANGS.
FARDEN'S SWORD FELL FROM HIS HAND AND DUG INTO THE GRASS.
LEAVE THIS PLACE,

I'VE COME TO FIND JERGAN! I MUST SPEAK WITH HIM!
JERGAN IS DEAD!
I DON'T WANT TO HURT YOU, JERGAN, I JUST WANT TO TALK!
HE DOESN'T LIVE HERE AND NEVER HAS SO LEAVE!
THE LYCAN SNARLED AND LEAPT TOWARDS THE MAGE. FARDEN SMACKED HIS WRISTS TOGETHER AND STAMPED HIS FOOT. A WALL OF FIRE BILLOWED OUT OF THE GROUND TOWARDS THE BEAST AND RIPPED THROUGH THE RAIN.
BUT WITH A ROAR THE AGILE CREATURE JUMPED OVER THE FLAMES AND BARED HIS TEETH IN THE RED GLOW.
HE SPRINTED TOWARDS THE MAGE AND SWUNG HIS CLAWS IN MAD ARCS.
FARDEN BLOCKED AND CUT STRAIGHT ACROSS JERGAN'S LEFT ARM. IT SENT THE LYCAN REELING BACKWARDS, YELPING, BUT HE MANAGED TO REACH OUT WITH ONE DEADLY PUNCH.
THE SWIPE CAUGHT FARDEN ON THE BREASTPLATE, WINDING HIM AND CRACKING A RIB.
YOU SHOULD TELL YOUR MAID NOT TO BUY YOU CHEAP SILVER MIRRORS, MAGE!
LOOK AT THIS!
WITH INCREDIBLE SPEED, FARDEN YANKED THE MIRROR FROM HIS CLOAK AND SHOWED IT TO THE LYCAN, LIFTING HIS LIGHT SPELL TO BLINDING LEVELS
LOOK!

THE LYCAN KICKED OUT AT FARDEN'S CHEST WITH A LONG HIND LEG. THE HUGE FOOT CAUGHT HIM HARD, RIGHT BELOW HIS THROAT, AND THE MAGE TUMBLED BACKWARDS WITH A CRY.
BUT AS HE FELL HE THREW THREE SMALL BOLTS OF BLISTERING FIRE AT JERGAN AND THE LYCAN STEPPED BACK QUICKLY, SWIPING FIRE FROM HIS FACE.
FARDEN ROLLED BACKWARDS SKILFULLY AND REGAINED HIS STANCE, THE WIND BLOWING THE SMELL OF CHARRED HAIR AND FLESH TO HIS KEEN NOSE.
FARDEN SUMMONED A DARK WELL OF STRENGTH AND THREW HIS ARMS OUT WILDLY. A RIPPLE OF MAGICK RIPPED THROUGH THE GROUND LIKE A CARPET BEING SHAKEN. ROCKS FLEW IN ALL DIRECTIONS.
LEAVE!
LET ME TALK TO JERGAN! I KNOW HE'S IN THERE SOMEWHERE.
JERGAN POUNCED AND FARDEN CLAPPED HIS HANDS TOGETHER WITH A BLAST OF FLAME. BUT THE LYCAN HAD BEEN TOO QUICK AND THE SPELL BROKE. FARDEN SKILFULLY REVERSED HIS GRIP AND RAKED THE SWORD ACROSS THE LYCAN'S SIDE. THE BEAST SNARLED AND LEAPT AWAY, BUT NOT BEFORE SCRAPING A CLAW ACROSS FARDEN'S CHEST, LUCKILY ONLY FINDING ARMOUR BENEATH.
JERGAN WAS GETTING TIRED AND HE KNEW IT, THE LYCAN'S SPELL WAS STARTING TO BREAK UNDER THE PRESSURE OF SUCH POWERFUL MAGICK. FARDEN WAS STARTING TO CRACK AS WELL, REMEMBERING DURNUS'S WORDS HE DUG HIS SWORD IN THE GROUND AND BEGAN TO CONCENTRATE ON THE WIND AROUND HIM.

FARDEN FORCED A VORTEX OF RAIN TO SPIN AROUND THE SNARLING LYCAN. THE WIND HOWLED KEENLY AND THE RAIN BATTERED JERGAN AS FARDEN SENT WALL AFTER WALL OF WIND AT THE BEAST.
DEFEATED, HE TURNED TAIL AND STUMBLED AWAY FROM FARDEN'S VORTEX SPELL. THE LYCAN RAN OFF INTO THE NIGHT, HOWLING AS HE DISAPPEARED.
HE LOWERED HIS HANDS AND COLLAPSED INTO THE SOAKING GRASS WITH EXHAUSTION.
FARDEN SWAYED ON HIS FEET AS THE WIND DIED BACK TO ITS NORMAL LEVEL.
MORNING BROUGHT IRON SKIES AND A LIGHT DRIZZLING RAIN.
WHEN DAWN FINALLY BROKE OVER THE MOORS, JERGAN HAD SLUNK BACK TO HIS HOVEL TO TRANSFORM. THE MAGE DETERMINEDLY STRODE FORWARD DOWN THE SLOPING HILL TOWARDS IT.
FARDEN LAY IN A TRANCE, HUNCHED UP WITH HIS CLOAK GATHERED AROUND HIM.
JERGAN! COME OUT HERE AND TALK! DON'T MAKE ME CUT YOUR HEAD OFF, YOU CUR!

FARDEN KICKED OPEN THE DOOR OF THE ROTTEN CABIN.
JERGAN! GET UP!
DON'T! DON'T KILL ME! PLEASE, I'LL DO WHATEVER YOU WANT!
YOU'D BETTER HAVE WHATEVER I CAME FOR, OR YOU'LL WISH I HAD KILLED YOU LAST NIGHT,
THAT WAS A LONG TIME AGO, MAGE. A VERY LONG TIME. I HAVE SPENT MY TORTURED YEARS TRYING TO FORGET THOSE PARTS OF MY LIFE. I'VE PUSHED THEM FROM ME, GIVEN THEM OVER TO THE BEAST. IF I CANNOT REMEMBER A LIFE BEFORE, BEFORE THIS, THEN HOW CAN I MISS IT?
WHAT COULD I POSSIBLY KNOW THAT'S OF ANY VALUE TO YOU?
WELL LET'S FIND OUT, SHALL WE? THREE DAYS AGO SOMETHING WAS STOLEN FROM MY PEOPLE,
A BOOK OF GREAT POWER, CLAIMED FROM THE SIRENS DURING THE WAR. YOU KNOW ANYTHING ABOUT IT?
JERGAN SIGHED.
I NEED MORE THAN THAT. WHAT WAS INSIDE THE BOOK?
YEARS BEFORE THE WAR, I WAS PART OF AN EXPEDITION THAT WAS SENT TO EXPLORE THE TAUSENBAR MOUNTAINS. AFTER THREE MONTHS WE FOUND A CAVE, AND IN THE DEPTHS OF THIS CAVE WE DISCOVERED AN OLD DARK ELF STRONGHOLD, DUG OUT OF THE ROCK, CRUMBLING WITH AGE. THE ELVES HAD ABANDONED IT OVERNIGHT, LEAVING EVERYTHING BEHIND. CLOTHES, FOOD, WEAPONS, AND BOOKS, THE KIND OF BOOKS THAT WE SCHOLARS CAN ONLY DREAM OF FINDING. THERE WAS ONE BOOK IN PARTICULAR, VERY OLD INDEED, COVERED IN DARK DRAGON SCALES.
ONCE OUR WIZARDS HAD FORCED IT OPEN, WE BEGAN TO EXAMINE ITS INCANTATIONS, SPELLS FOR SUMMONING MONSTERS, CREATURES, AND SPIRITS FROM THE OTHER SIDE. AT THE COST OF A FEW WIZARDS, WE EVEN MANAGED TO SUMMON A FEW, AND THOSE FELL CREATURES DID ANYTHING WE TOLD THEM.
THE MOST POWERFUL SPELL IN THE MANUAL WAS FOR SUMMONING A MOST ANCIENT AND TERRIFYING MONSTER, CALLED "THE MOUTHS OF DARKNESS". SOME SORT OF CROSSBREED OF DAEMON AND DRAGON. NONE OF OUR WIZARDS COULD STOMACH ITS WORDS. JUST UTTERING THE KEYS SCARED THEM WITLESS. FARFALLEN WAS FURIOUS WHEN HE LEARNED OF THE SPELL, AND OF THE CREATURE. HE HAD THE MANUAL BANISHED TO SOUTHERN NELSKA, AND THAT WAS THE LAST I EVER SAW OF IT. I WENT ON TO EXPLORE THE ICE WASTES...

JERGAN SNIFFED PITIFULLY. THE MAGE REACHED INSIDE HIS TRAVEL BAG AND PULLED OUT TWO BRUISED APPLES. HE TOSSED ONE TO JERGAN.
BUT IF NOBODY CAN CAST THAT SPELL, WHY STEAL IT?
HE MUSED AS HE CRUNCHED ON HIS APPLE, TURNING OVER IDEAS IN HIS HEAD
I DIDN'T SAY NOBODY COULD CAST IT. THERE ARE PERHAPS A FEW IN EMANESKA THAT COULD. LIKE THOSE WHO SENT YOU.
IT CAN'T HAVE BEEN ONE OF THE ARKMAGES. THAT'S ABSURD.
THEN I SUPPOSE I'LL BE HUNTING DRAGONS NEXT.
IT'S NOT JUST A MATTER OF BEING ABLE TO HANDLE THE SPELL. THIS SPELL REQUIRES A POWERFUL SOURCE OF DARK MAGICK, TO HELP THE BEAST CROSS OVER. LIKE THE WELLS THE DARK ELVES BUILT TO HOUSE THEIR MAGICK. MUCH LIKE THE BOOK YOU CARRY, MAGE.
...LAKES OF MAGICK BELOW PATHS UNTRODDEN. YES, EVERYBODY KNOWS THAT OLD RIDDLE. THE ELF WELLS ARE ALL GONE, LOST TO TIME.
IF YOU'RE GOING TO GO THEN I WOULD ASK ONE FAVOUR OF YOU. IF YOU DO COME ACROSS ANY OF THE DRAGONS, THEN AT LEAST TELL THEM THAT I'M ALIVE, AND NOT DEAD. THAT'S ALL I ASK.
THEN IF IT WASN'T ANY OF THE ARKA, THAT MEANS THE WAR IS FAR FROM OVER.
DON'T FORGET, FARDEN, THE EXISTENCE OF THIS BOOK IS NOT COMMON KNOWLEDGE. DARK ELVES ARE OUT OF THE QUESTION, SO THE THIEF IS EITHER SIREN, OR ARKA. THAT'S THE TRUTH OF IT.
ARE YOU SURE? I'VE ALWAYS BELIEVED THERE MIGHT BE A CLUE TO THE LAST ELF WELL IN THE OLD DRAGON'S MEMORIES.
I WILL. THANK YOU JERGAN, FOR YOUR HELP. I UNDERSTAND YOU DIDN'T ASK FOR THIS, FOR THE LIFE OF A LYCAN, AND I HOPE THAT YOU SURVIVE IT A WHILE LONGER.
GOOD LUCK...
BEINNH
... AND WITH THAT THE MAGE LEFT, JOGGING ACROSS THE HILLS, BACK TOWARDS BEINNH, AND THE ARKABBEY TO THE NORTH.

NIGHT HAD ONCE AGAIN FALLEN UPON THE MURKY STREETS OF BEINNH. ALL WAS SILENT, SAVE FOR A FEW DRUNKARDS AND A LIGHT HAMMERING, RINGING BETWEEN THE ALLEYWAYS.
THE THIN OLD BLACKSMITH PUT HIS HAMMER DOWN, AND STRETCHED HIS ACHING HANDS WITH A SMIRK, HE PLUCKED A HANDFUL OF COINS FROM HIS POUCH AND TAPPED THEM AGAINST HIS TEETH.
SELLING OLD SPEARS FOR NEW HAD BAGGED HIM A FINE BIT OF GOLD. ALL THEY NEEDED WERE A BIT OF SPIT AND A HAMMER'S KISS.
SUDDENLY, THE DOOR FLEW OPEN WITH A LOUD BANG, A STRANGER STOOD IN THE DOORWAY,
YOU CAN KEEP YOUR MONEY OLD THIEF. BUT YOU CAN HAVE YOUR MIRROR BACK!
YOU LIED TO ME ABOUT THE SILVER MIRROR, AND I WARNED YOU WHAT WOULD HAPPEN.
I REMEMBER YER, I REMEMBER! I'M SORRY! I'LL DO WHATEVER YOU WANT, ER, YOU CAN 'AVE YER MONEY BACK I SWEAR! JUS' PLEASE DON'T KILL ME...
THE SMITH CRUMPLED TO THE EARTH IN A FLURRY OF GLASS AND SPIT AND WENT SILENT. THE MIRROR SKIPPED AND SKITTERED OVER THE DUSTY FLOOR AND COLLIDED WITH THE STONE WALL OF THE FORGE WITH A CLANG.
THE MAGE LEFT WITHOUT A SOUND. THE CLOUDS HAD OPENED AND A HEAVY RAIN SOAKED THE TOWN. LIGHTNING FLICKERED ONTHE HORIZON, SIGN OF ANOTHER STORM APPROACHING. FARDEN LOOKED NORTH, AND PULLED HIS HOOD LOW.
INSCRIPTION:
" THOSE OF SPECIAL CIRCUMSTANCE, CAN FIND THEMSELVES ALONE, BY THE FIELD THE HOUSE THE MOUNTAIN CRAG, THE BLOOD BEGETS THE BONE, FRIEND OF FOES, AND FAIR THEE WELL, WATCH OUT FOR SHADOWS BLACK, FOR DARKNESS COMES TO THEM TOO SOON, A WING'D TEETH, BARED BLADES, AND TRAP. THEY WANT WHAT IS DIFFERENT, BUT AS ALL, WE WANT THE SAME, THUS BLOOD BECOMES THE BIRTHRIGHT, AND THY NIGHT BECOMES THY SHAME. THEY JUDGE US BY THE DIFFERENCE, THEY JUDGE US FROM THY TEETH. BUT WE WATCH THEIR NECKS, WE'LL STRING THEM UP, AND LEAVE THEM THERE TO BLEED. "
VAMPYRE POEM OF UNKNOWN ORIGIN.
BLACKSMITH
100% GENUINE

DURNUS WAS DOZING IN HIS LOFT ROOM. HIS SLEEPY MIND WAS CHURNING OVER THOUGHTS OF WAR, AND COUNTRIES, KINGDOMS AND TRAITORS AND OF THE LEGENDS OF OLD.
THE RAIN HAMMERED ON THE STAINED GLASS WINDOW. IT WOULD BE NIGHT SOON, AND THERE WAS NOTHING BETTER THAN HUNTING IN THE RAIN.
PROPPED UP IN A CORNER OF HIS ROOM WAS A TALL ARCHWAY MADE FROM BLACK STONE AND METAL SCAFFOLDING. THE CONTRAPTION LEANT OVER A LECTERN HOLDING A VERY THICK BROWN BOOK. THE BLACK STONE FLICKERED IN THE CANDLELIGHT.
SUDDENLY. . .
FARDEN !
WATER.
YOU'VE BEEN GONE FOR ALMOST A WEEK, WE WERE STARTING TO GET ANXIOUS.
FARDEN, HOLD STILL.
BY THE GODS THAT FEELS BETTER. I'VE NEVER RUN THAT FAR THAT FAST BEFORE.

THAT FELT INCREDIBLE...
WHY HAVE YOU NEVER DONE THAT BEFORE?
JOLTING THE BRAIN LIKE THAT TOO MANY TIMES CAN KILL A MAN. EVEN ONE AS STRONG AS YOU.
I HAVE NEWS.
WELL LET'S GET TO IT! WHAT HAPPENED?
WELL, I FOUND JERGAN WHERE YOU SAID HE'D BE, SOUTH OF BEINNH AND, FOR A HERMIT, HE WASN'T AT ALL SHY WHEN IT CAME TO TRYING TO KILL ME.
ANYWAY, IN SHORT, YOU WERE RIGHT. JERGAN AND THE SIRENS FOUND THE BOOK IN THE TAUSENBAR MOUNTAINS.
THEY CAST THE SPELLS IN IT?
THAT'S WHAT JERGAN SAID, AND FOR SOME REASON I TRUST HIM. THEY WENT THROUGH IT SYSTEMATICALLY FROM COVER TO COVER, AND THEIR WIZARDS TESTED THE DAEMONS. JERGAN THINKS THAT'S WHY SOMEONE WOULD STEAL THE BOOK, TO GET AT THE POWERFUL BEASTS HIDDEN IN ITS PAGES.
BUT THE ARKA HAVE FOUGHT DAEMONS AND ANCIENT BEASTS BEFORE, YOU WERE THERE FIVE YEARS AGO, WHEN THE MINOTAURS CAME OUT OF EFJAR WASTES? WHY SHOULD THIS BOOK BE ANY DIFFERENT?
HE SAID THIS BOOK HELD ONE SPELL THAT THE DRAGON-RIDERS FEARED SO MUCH THEY WERE NEVER ABLE TO CAST IT. THEY NEVER FOUND OUT HOW BUT IT WAS SOMETHING THAT SCARED THE SIRENS AND THEIR DRAGONS TO DEATH., APPARENTLY A TERRIFYING BEAST, THE "MOUTHS OF DARKNESS". THEY WERE FOOLISH.
FOOLISH INDEED. THEY WOULD NEED A GREAT SOURCE OF MAGICK... PERHAPS LIKE ONE OF THE DARK ELF WELLS?
EXACTLY!
DURNUS, CAN YOU SEND ME TO THE QUICKDOOR AT THE SPIRE?
THIS IS DIRE NEWS, FARDEN. WE HAVE TO SUPPOSE THAT WHOEVER STOLE THE MANUAL WISHES TO RELEASE THIS BEAST ON THE WORLD. WE NEED TO GET YOU TO KRAUSLUNG WITH ALL SPEED. I'LL NEED MOST OF THE NIGHT TO PREPARE THE QUICKDOOR TO THE CITADEL, YOU NEED TO REST.
I DONT SEE WHY NOT.
THANK YOU.

ELESSI WAS WANDERING THE CORRIDORS OF THE ARKABBEY TOWER. ARTER HEARING A RUMOUR THAT FARDEN WAS BACK, SHE HAD GONE LOOKING FOR HIM WITH ANGST IN HER HEART.
NOW IT WAS LATE AND HER SEARCH OF HIS ROOM AND CAVERNOUS DINING HALL HAD BEEN FRUITLESS.
THE EARNEST MAID SKIPPED UP THE STEPS TO THE TRAINING HALLS NEAR THE BELL TOWER, HOLDING HER SKIRTS ABOVE HER SHOES AND LISTENING TO THE WOODEN DOORS OF LOCKED QUARTERS AND ROOMS HOME TO SLEEPING SOLDIERS.
YELLOW TORCHLIGHT SPLIT FROM A DOOR HALF-CLOSED AT THE END OF THE CORRIDOR.
ELESSI CREPT FORWARD.
THE CHAMBERMAID WAS TRANSFIXED : HER EYES LOCKED IN A MESMERISED STARE.

THERE, STANDING SHIRTLESS AND SWEATING, WAS FARDEN, THROWING BOLT AFTER BOLT OF FIRE AT A WOODEN MAN-SHAPED TARGET. IT ROCKED AND BUCKLED UNDER THE POWERFUL BLASTS OF MAGICK.
ELESSI'S EYES WERE FIXATED ON FARDEN'S BACK. LINES AND LINES OF THIN BLACK SCRIPT COVERERD THE MAGE'S SHOULDERS AND LOWER BACK, PUNCTUATED BY SWIRLING ELEGANT LINES AND SPIRALS CLAMBERING OVER HIS COLLARBONE AND SHOULDER BLADES. FOUR SYMBOLS RAN ALONG HIS SPINE, RUNES WITH SHAPES AND STRANGE INTERWOVEN WORDS. ELESSI COULDN'T HELP BUT NOTICE THE DARK FACES OF TELLING BRUISES RUNNING THROUGH THE BLACK LETTERING AND EVERY TIME THE MAGICK SURGED THROUGH HIS BODY THE WORDS FLASHED AND GLOWED SPORADICALLY. LIGHTING UP ALL OVER HIS SKIN.
THE WINTER SUN HOVERED NEAR THE HORIZON BEHIND THE TREES. HIDING BEHIND THE LEAFLESS BRANCHES OF THE FOREST OF DURN.
THAT NIGHT, ELESSI DREAMT OF WOUNDED GHOSTS, AND HULKING MONSTERS, OF DEEP CAVES AND OF FIRE BURNING UNDER HER SHEETS. SLEEP RAN FROM HER AND ELESSI WOKE WITH RED EYES AND DRIPPING WITH COLD SWEAT.
DURNUS REPOSED IN A WOODEN CHAIR NEAR A DESK, EYES CLOSED AND DOSING.
FARDEN. HMM. WHAT TIME IS IT?
FARDEN WALKED GENTLY UP TO HIIM AND PUT A GENTLE HAND ON THE OLD MAN'S SHOULDER.
JUST BEFORE NOON, IT'LL BE AFTERNOON IN MANESMARK BY NOW.
RIGHT!

THE VAMPYRE RAMBLED AWAY AS HE LEAFED THROUGH THE PAGES, PREPARING THE NEXT SPELL.
IT'S ALL ABOUT PATIENCE, MY GOOD MAGE. THINK OF IT AS TRYING TO OPEN AND CLOSE A WINDOW A THOUSAND MILES AWAY, WITH NO MORE THAN A ROPE AND A LONG POLE.
YOU KNOW I DON'T UNDERSTAND THIS TIME AND SPACE MAGICK, MY OLD FRIEND, THAT'S YOUR AREA OF EXPERTISE NOT MINE.
THAT DOESN'T REALLY HELP.
I CAN SMELL BLOOD ON YOUR SWORD. . .
WHO ELSE DID YOU FIGHT BESIDES JERGAN?
DON'T GET SLOPPY, FARDEN. YOU ARE AN INSTRUMENT OF THE ARKA FIRST AND FOREMOST, A FINELY TUNED WEAPON OF PRECISION AND TACT. THERE ARE CONSEQUENCES FOR POOR DESCISIONS, MAGE, BEAR THEM IN MIND NEXT TIME YOU DRAW YOUR SWORD.
SOME PEOPLE JUST DONT LISTEN.
I WATCHED YOUR UNCLE GO DOWN THIS VIOLENT PATH A LONG TIME AGO, AND LOOK WHERE IT GOT HIM. THIS IS THE LAST TIME I'LL TELL YOU.
. . . I WILL.
FARDEN FELT THE ICY BLAST OF THE QUICKDOOR ON HIS SKIN AND RAN HIS HANDS OVER THE TINGLING THRESHOLD.
AS HE LIFTED HIS FOOT THE DOOR SUDDENLY GRABBED HIM IN A VICE-LIKE GRIP AND DRAGGED HIM FORWARDS INTO A BLINDING WHITE TUNNEL OF LIGHT AND NOISE.

"IT WAS AT THIS TIME THAT THE SCRIBE CAME TO US, THE SECRET BEHIND A WRITTEN'S STRENGTH, AND A GREAT AND POWERFUL WING OF THE MAGICK COUNCIL CAME TO EXIST, CHARGED TO WATCH OVER THE DARK FORCES LEFT BEHIND BY THE ELVES. THE PEERS OF THE ARKA FACTIONS WERE NOW UNDER A GREAT DUTY; TO SEE THAT THE POWERS OF GOOD WERE EXCERCISED IN THE WILD LANDS OF EMANESKA, AND THAT DIRECTION AND ORDER WERE BROUGHT TO THE PEOPLE."
"THIS WAS OF COURSE, BEFORE THE GREED OF THE RICH SOUGHT TO PERVERT THE POWER OF THE TWO THRONES, WHEN ONE BY ONE THE MEMBERS OF THE COUNCIL TURNED THEIR MINDS FROM JUSTICE AND GOOD, AND WANTED FOR GOLD AND POWER INSTEAD."
ARKMAGE OLFAR, WRITING IN THE YEAR 78

ARKA SOLDIERS WATCHED AS THE MANESMARK QUICKDOOR RUMBLED AND FIZZLED WITH MAGICK.
FARDEN STUMBLED ONTO THE WET FROZEN GRASS OF THE MANESMARK HILLSIDE.
I'D LIKE TO SEE YOU TRY TO LAND MORE GRACEFULLY.
THE DIZZY MAGE SAID NO MORE AND WALKED FORWARD TO LOOK OUT ACROSS THE STUNNING COUNTRYSIDE THAT HE HAD KNOWN AS A BOY.
THE LANDSCAPE WAS STILL AS BREATHTAKING AS HE REMEMBERED. THE TALL ÖSSFEN MOUNTAILNS STRETCHED OUT FOR MILES AND MILES, THEIR SNOW-CAPPED PEAKS SCRAPING AT THE HEAVY GREY CLOUDS WITH THEIR ROCKY TEETH.

TO THE NORTH HE COULD SEE THE DEADLY SLOPES OF LOKKI, THE TALLEST MOUNTAIN IN EMANESKA. BENEATH HIM ON THE STEEP HILLSIDES VILLAGES SAT WREATHED IN WOOD SMOKE, PEEKING OUT OF THE SNOWDRIFTS.

FARDEN LOOKED DOWN THE HILL AT MANESMARK, THE TRADITIONAL HOME OF THE ARKA'S FIGHTING FORCES. SCATTERED MEMORIES RAN LIKE RABBITS THROUGH THE FIELDS OF THE MAGE'S MIND AS HE WALKED ACROSS THE HILLSIDE.

MANESMARK WAS THE LONG-ESTABLISHED HOME OF THE WRITTEN AND OF THE SCHOOL WHERE FARDEN AND EVERY OTHER MAGE STUDIED.

HE COULD STILL SMELL THE STRANGE, EVER-PRESENT BURNING SMELL OF THE PLACE, FEEL THE ROUGH WOOD OF THE FLOORS, THE BEDS...

TASTE THE WATERY YELLOW GRUEL.

THE SCHOOL OF THE WRITTEN HAD BEEN A CRUEL WORLD OF BULLYING, SPELLS, AND CONSTANT FEAR. MANY OF HIS CLASSMATES HAD DIED ALONG THE WAY...

VICIOUS COMPETITION PLAGUED THE PRESTIGIOUS SCHOOL. FARDEN HAD BARELY MADE IT INTO THE FINAL CUT. HE REMEMBERED STANDING BEFORE THE ELDERS, BEATEN AND BRUISED, PULSATING WITH MAGICK ON HIS FINAL DAY, FEELING THE BLOOD RUN DOWN HIS BROW AND HEARING HIS NAME IN THEIR STERN LIPS.

EVERY MOMENT HAD BEEN TORTURE, BUT IT HAD MADE HIM A MAN, TAUGHT HIM THE TRUE FACE OF MAGICK, AND SHOWN HIM THE WILD NATURE BEHIND EMANESKA.

VICTIMS OF AN 'ACCIDENTAL' KNIFE THRUST...

OR PERHAPS CAUGHT BY A WAYWARD SPELL.

FARDEN WAS SURE NOTHING HAD CHANGED.

'FRAID YOU CAN'T GO IN SIRE, TOO MANY ALREADY IN THERE.

HANGING IN THE MIDDLE OF THE SPIRE'S ATRIUM WAS A COLLOSAL DRAGON SCALE SUSPENDED IN THE AIR BY GREAT STEEL CHAINS. IT QUIVERED WITH ENERGY AND WAS MAKING A DEEP WHINING SOUND. TOO MANY WRITTEN MAGES IN THE SPIRE AT ONE TIME COULD SEND THE OTHER MEN MAD FROM THE PURE POWER OF THE RAW MAGICK. THE BEATEN DRAGON SCALE WAS LIKE A WARNING BELL FOR THE SPIRE.

THE MAGE SHRUGGED TO HIMSELF: KRAUSLUNG COULD WAIT FOR A WHILE.

AS SOON AS IT CAME CLOSE ENOUGH, SHE QUICKLY UNTIED THE WOODEN CANISTER FROM ITS LEG.
CHESKA WAS STANDING IN HER ROOM WATCHING THE MESSENGER HAWK FLUTTER AROUND HER WINDOWSILL.
THREE HASTILY SCRIBBLED WORDS WAS ALL SHE NEEDED TO READ.
CHESKA HELD THE NOTE IN HER HAND AND CONCENTRATED HARD WITH MUTTERING LIPS. THERE WAS A BRIEF FLASH OF LIGHT AND THE NOTE BECAME ASH IN HER HAND.
THE SOUND OF THE SCALE BELOW HER REACHED HER EARS AND SHE IMMEDIATELY TURNED TO LEAVE HER MODEST ROOM.
AFTERNOON CHESKA.
OH, BRIM, I WAS JUST LEAVING,
WELL I'M GOING TO THE MARKET, WE CAN WALK IF YOU WANT?

THE TWO FRIENDS STRODE THROUGH THE SPIRE'S CORRIDORS TOGETHER.

IT WAS COMMON KNOWLEDGE THAT CHESKA WAS THE DAUGHTER OF BANE, THE KING OF THE POWERFUL SKOLGARD EMPIRE IN THE NORTHEAST. AND THAT MADE HER A PRINCESS. FOR HER TO BE EVEN LIVING WITH THE ARKA, LET ALONE PRACTISING THEIR DANGEROUS MAGICK WAS A MASSIVE POLITICAL STEP FOR BOTH COUNTRIES.
SHE HAD IMMERSED HERSELF IN THE BRUTAL WORLD OF MAGICK. FARDEN HAD TO ADMIT, SHE WAS GOOD, AND IT HAD MADE THEIR LITTLE AFFAIR EVEN MORE EXCITING AND DANGEROUS.

THE MAGE'S EYES SCANNED THE THRONGS OF PEOPLE MILLING AROUND, LOOKING FOR SOMEONE IN PARTICULAR. SHE MUST HAVE HEARD THE SCALE RING, FARDEN THOUGHT.

FARDEN WAS QUICKLY GETTING BORED. THE SOLITARY MAGE HAD ALWAYS BEEN QUIET AROUND MOST OF THE OTHERS, PREFERRING HIS OWN COMPANY, AND IT WAS NO SECRET IN THE SPIRE THAT PEOPLE THOUGHT HIM DANGEROUS AND WILD.

WELL WELL! LOOK WHAT THE GRYPHON DRAGGED IN!

AHEM...

HUH?. . . OH,

. . .THEN HE SAW HER.

OH, FARDEN, YOU REMEMBER BRIM DON'T YOU?

WE'VE MET A FEW TIMES BEFORE, GOOD TO SEE YOU AGAIN.
OFFICIAL BUSINESS IN KRAUSLUNG. I HAVE TO BE HEADING THERE SOON.
YOU'RE RIGHT,
TELL ME THAT'S NOT WHAT I THINK IT IS. . .
YOU TOO SIR, WHAT BRINGS YOU TO MANESMARK?
SHE PULLED BACK HER SLEEVES AND REVEALED A RED BAND OF METAL WRAPPED AROUND HER SLENDER WRIST, IT WAS A FJORTLA, A BRACELET THAT TRADITIONALLY MARKED A TRAINEE FOR BEING WRITTEN, A DANGEROUS THREE DAY TATTOOING PROCESS THAT ONLY HALF OF THE CANDIDATES SURVIVED.
WE BOTH GOT CHOSEN AND WE'LL BE WRITTEN IN LESS THAN A MONTH!
BOTH OF YOU?
DON'T EVEN START WITH THAT VULNERABLE WOMAN SHIT.
WALK WITH ME A WHILE?
I'LL MEET YOU LATER IN THE MARKET, BRIM.
BOTH OF US,
GREAT,
ARE YOU ACTUALLY SERIOUS?
STILL WEARING THE PRESENT I GOT YOU?
NO, NOT HERE FARDEN
BE CAREFUL IN KRAUSLUNG.
ME? BE CAREFUL?
IF WE GET CAUGHT THEY'LL THROW YOU IN THE STOCKS.
THEY WOULDN'T DARE.
I'LL FIND YOU.
POLITICS. . .
OH DON'T BE A HYPOCITE, FARDEN. YOU SAID YOU COULDN'T WAIT TO GO THROUGH WITH IT WHEN THEY CHOSE YOU.
IT'S JUST DANGEROUS, CHESKA, AND YOU KNOW. . .
POLITICS AND RULES!
I KNOW WHAT?
YOU KNOW. . .
IT WAS LAW THAT NO TWO WRITTEN CAN COME TOGETHER.
BOOT

FARDEN DEPARTED DOWN THE STEEP HILL AWAY FROM MANESMARK AND CONTINUED HIS JOURNEY THROUGH THE MOUNTAINS.

A FEW HOURS' WALK FROM MANESMARK, NESTLED IN A DEEP VALLEY BETWEEN THE TWIN PEAKS OF URSUFEL AND HARDJA, LAY THE IMMENSE CITADEL OF KRAUSLUNG, CAPITAL CITY OF THE ARKA, HOME OF THE ARKATHEDRAL AND TO THE RULING POWERS OF THE MAGICK COUNCIL.

THE HOODED MAGE STRODE OVER THE FROZEN GRASS OF THE VALLEY, STARING UP AT THE TWO STEEP MOUNTAINS EITHER SIDE OF HIM. THEY TOWERED OVER THE CITY WALLS. THE IMMENSE RAMPARTS OF KRAUSLUNG FILLED THE GAP BETWEEN THE TWO PEAKS, USING THEIR CLIFFS AS A SOLID FOUNDATION FOR THEIR THICK STONE DEFENCES.

A STREAM OF TRAVELLERS AND CITY FOLK FLOWED THROUGH THE MASSIVE MAIN GATE. STONE BATTLEMENTS CRESTED THE WALLS, AND FROM THERE A SMALL ARMY OF GUARDS WATCHED OVER THE ARRIVING VISITORS AND PEERED DOWN FROM THEIR RECLUSIVE ARROW SLITS.

THE LONG AND UNEASY CEASEFIRE WITH THE SIRENS HAD MADE THE ARKA GUARDS WARY AND SUSPICIOUS OVER THE YEARS, EVER FEARING THE SHADOW OF A DRAGON OR A SIREN SPY.

THE GUARDS EYED FARDEN WARILY FOR A MOMENT AS HE PASSED BENEATH THEM, AND THEN, RECOGNISING WHAT HE WAS, THEY LOOKED AWAY QUICKLY TO GLARE AT THE NEXT PERSON.

THE MAGE MADE HIS WAY DEEPER INTO THE VALLEY AND DOWN INTO THE CITADEL. IN KRAUSLUNG EVERYONE SEEMED TO LIVE ON TOP OR UNDERNEATH EVERYONE ELSE.
THE BUILDINGS OF KRAUSLUNG WERE PILED STOREY UPON STOREY, UNTIL EACH SEEMED TO LEAN AGAINST THE NEXT...
AHEAD OF HIM WAS THE MAIN CITY, AND FROM HIS VANTAGE POINT AT THE GATE HE COULD SEE THE WHOLE OF KRAUSLUNG SPREAD OUT AHEAD OF HIM LIKE AN INTRICATE CARPET. FARDEN JOINED THE SLOW MOVING THRONGS OF PEOPLE HEADING TOWARDS THE CITY,
MERCHANTS AT THE ROADSIDE CALLED OUT TO THE PASSERS-BY HOPING TO MAKE A FEW MORE SALES BEFORE NIGHT FINALLY FELL.
...MAKING THE STREETS SEEM LIKE THE DARKENED ARTERIES AND CAPILLARIES OF SOME IMMENSE LIVING THING.
DOWN ON THE STREETS IT WAS NOISY; THE GUTTERS WERE FULL OF WATER FROM THE WINTER SNOWS AND GODS KNOWS WHAT ELSE. PEOPLE LEANT OUT OF WINDOWS AND SHOUTED TO OTHERS DOWN IN THE STREET, WHILE OTHERS GAMBLED AND BARTERED IN THE NARROW ALLEYWAYS.
FARDEN LOVED IT. HERE NOBODY PAID ATTENTION TO HIM, HE COULD MELT INTO THE DARK ALLEYWAYS AND MARKET STALLS AND NOBODY WOULD LOOK TWICE AT THE SHADY MAGE. EVEN THE PICKPOCKETING CHILDREN IGNORED HIM, KNOWING BETTER THAN TO MESS WITH A WRITTEN.

LEANING AGAINST THE PRECIPITOUS WALLS OF HARDJA, STOOD THE ARKATHEDRAL.

IT HAD BEEN MANY MONTHS SINCE FARDEN HAD BEEN HERE LAST AND THE MAGE HAD ALMOST FORGOTTEN THE IMPRESSIVE VIEW.

HERE WAS THE THROBBING HEART OF THE ARKA, WHERE THE BALANCE OF MAGICK WAS KEPT IN CHECK AND THE COUNCIL PLAYED OUT THEIR GAME OF CHESS WITH THE WORLD.

TO HIS LEFT A GROUP OF FINE LADIES, THEIR FACES PAINTED AND THEIR HAIR TIED UP HIGH, RAN GLOVED HANDS OVER JEWELLERY AND ORNAMENTS AT A SHOP WINDOW.

"POTIONS, LOTIONS AND NOTIONS, MAGICKAL REMEDIES FOR ALL! VIGTOR URTT: PURVEYOR OF BLADES AND POINTY WEAPONS! FINE CLOTHES FOR FINE WOMEN!" "NO BEGGARS ALLOWED."

A FEW OF THE WOMEN HAD THEIR PET GEESE BY THEIR SIDE. THE FAT BIRDS WERE DECORATED IN THE SAME COLOURS AS THEIR OWNERS' DRESSES. THEY HONKED QUIETLY AND IMPATIENTLY WADDLED FROM SIDE TO SIDE. FARDEN SMILED.

THIS WAS HOW THE CITY WAS, AND MORE SO IN RECENT YEARS THAN EVER BEFORE. THE POOR LIVED BELOW THE RICH, SO CLOSE AND YET SO FAR, NEITHER CROSSING THE GAP BETWEEN THE CLASSES BUT WILLING TO LIVE IN ROUGH HARMONY AS LONG AS THEIR PEACEFUL WAY OF LIFE WAS MAINTAINED.

"SEE I THINK THOSE ARKMAGES IS SNEAKY, WHY ELSE WOULD THEY KEEP US ALL OUT OF THEIR PRETTY TOWER, SECRETIVE LIKE. I HEAR THAT THERE HELYARD BLOKE CAN CHANGE THE WEATHER. MAKE IT RAIN AND ALL THAT? SEE NOW THAT SCARES ME. IF IT WERE UP TO ME, I WOULD HAVE US PEOPLE RUNNING THINGS, MAKING SURE WE'RE NOT UP TO NO MISCHIEF AND ALL. WE'RE THE ONES WHO KNOWS BEST." "WHAT, THE WAR? WELL THAT WAS ALL ABOUT GOLD OR LAND OR SOMETHING, YEH IT WAS DEFINITELY ABOUT GOLD..." OVERHEARD DURING A CONVERSATION IN A KRAUSLUNG TAVERN

AS FARDEN CLIMBED THE STEPS OF THE ARKATHEDRAL, A LOUD VOICE RANG OUT THROUGH THE MARBLE CORRIDOR.
FARDEN!
THE MAGE TURNED TO SEE A FAMILIAR FACE CREASING WITH A BIG SMILE AND AN OUTSTRETCHED HAND COMING TOWARDS HIM.
UNDERMAGE, ALWAYS A PLEASURE.
IT'S BEEN TOO LONG, FARDEN, TOO LONG AND YOU CAN DISPENSE WITH THAT UNDERMAGE RUBBISH, YOU KNOW ME BETTER THAN THAT.
I CAN SEE YOU HAVEN'T CHANGED, STILL PLAYING THE POLITICIAN AS USUAL.
THIS IS A DARK TIME FOR US FARDEN. I HOPE YOU HAVE SOME GOOD NEWS.
I HAVE NEWS, BUT WHETHER IT'S GOOD OR NOT WILL BE UP TO THE ARKMAGES AND YOU.
VICE WAS AN OLD FRIEND AND A POWERFUL MENTOR TO FARDEN, AND HE HAD KNOWN HIM ALMOST ALL HIS LIFE. NOW A WAR HERO, VICE HAD BEEN A LOWLY INSTRUCTOR, BUT STEP BY STEP HE HAD CLIMBED THROUGH THE RANKS TO SIT BESIDE THE TWO ARKMAGES, THE POWERFUL HELYARD AND THE WISE ADDREN.
VICE HAD BEEN ONE OF THE BEST AT THE SCHOOL, AND HAD TAUGHT FARDEN MANY OF HIS TRICKS AND SPELLS. BUT HE WASN'T A WRITTEN, AND HE COULDN'T BEGIN TO COMPARE HIMSELF TO THE POWER OF THE ARKMAGES.
THE TRAGEDY AT ARFELL HAS HIT US HARD. IT'S BAD ENOUGH HAVING OUR VALUABLE SCHOLARS BRUTALLY MURDERED BUT TO HAVE A DANGEROUS BOOK TAKEN FROM OUR SAFE HANDS IS MUCH WORSE.
I AGREE.
THEY ARRIVED AT A WIDE GILDED DOOR, ONE THAT FARDEN HAD SELDOM WALKED THROUGH. GUARDS FLANKED THE DOOR IN FULL CEREMONIAL ARMOUR.
LET'S GO IN.

FARDEN STEPPED INTO THE GREAT HALL AND TRIED TO KEEP HIS MOUTH FROM HANGING OPEN. IT WAS LIKE STEPPING INTO A WHITE AND GOLD CAVERN, WITH BEAMS AND GILDED RAFTERS THAT RESEMBLED THE RIBS OF SOME HUGE FOSSILISED FOREST. HE SCANNED THE MEN AND WOMEN AND PLACES FROZEN FOREVER IN THE PATTERNS OF THE COLOURED GLASS, THEIR FACES EMOTIONLESS AND REGAL.
THE MAGE KEPT WALKING AND FOLLOWED VICE TO THE BACK OF THE GREAT HALL. ALMOST A HUNDERED PEOPLE STOOD AROUND THEM, LOITERING AMONGST THE PILLARS AND BENCHES, CLAD IN ROBES OF VARIOUS HUES, TALKING IN LOW VOICES AND POINTING AT THE MAGE. FARDEN IGNORED THEM.
AT THE END OF THE ROOM STOOD THREE GIANT CHAIRS. HERE SAT THE ARKMAGES HELYARD AND ADREN, RULERS OF THE ARKA AND THE HEADS OF THE MAGICK COUNCIL, POWRFUL AND WISE AND BEYOND CONTESTATION.
ADDREN SPOKE FIRST. THOUGH THIN AND AGING THE POWERFUL MAN STILL WORE THE LONG GREEN AND GOLD ARKMAGE'S ROBE WITH PRIDE AND A STRICT POSTURE. HE HADN'T CHANGED A BIT SINCE FARDEN HAD LAST SEEN HIM.
WELCOME, FARDEN, TO THE ARKATHEDRAL. I TRUST YOUR JOURNEY WAS SWIFT?
IT WAS, YOUR MAGE.
TELL US YOUR FINDINGS THEN, FARDEN. IF THIS NEWS IS AS URGENT AS I'M TOLD, YOUD BEST BE OUT WITH IT.
FOR HIS AGE, HELYARD WAS SURPRISINGLY THICK- SET AND MUSCULAR, ECHOES OF A LONG LIFE SPENT ON THE BATTLEFIELD. THE AUSTERE HELYARD SIGHED THEATRICALLY.

FARDEN NODDED ONCE MORE AND TOOK A BREATH. HE SPOKE SLOWLY AND WITH A MEASURED TONE, STRIVING TO REMEMBER EVERY DETAIL, LIKE DURNUS HAD TOLD HIM. HE WAS UNUSUALLY NERVOUS IN FRONT OF THESE OLD MEN.
YES, LORD HELYARD. THE BOOK STOLEN FROM ARFELL IS AN OLD DARK ELF MANUAL, A SPELL BOOK FOR SUMMONING DAEMONS AND BEASTS FROM DARK PLACES. A FEW DAYS AGO I TRAVLLED FURTHER SOUTH INTO ALBION TO FIND A SIREN HERMIT CALLED JERGAN. HE HAD BEEN PART OF A TEAM OF WIZARDS AND SCHOLARS THAT FIRST DISCOVERED THE BOOK. IN AN ANCIENT ELF FORTRESS IN THE MOUNTAINS, THE SAME TEAM THAT WENT ON TO DECIPHER AND CAST SOME OF ITS SPELLS.
JERGAN SPOKE OF THE WORST AND MOST POWERFUL OF THEM ALL, SOMETHING THEY HAD CALLED "THE MOUTH" OR "MOUTHS OF DARKNESS" THEY TRIED, AND FAILED TO SUMMON IT, AND BEFORE THEY GOT ANY FURTHER, THE OLD DRAGON HAD THE BOOK BANISHED TO A SECRET LOCATION IN SOUTHERN NELSKA, AND NEVER SPOKE OF IT AGAIN.
NO YOUR MAGE, JERGAN HAS BECOME A PATHETIC HERMIT, NOTHING BUT A SLAVE TO HIS CURSE. HE WAS BITTEN YEARS AGO ON THE ICE FIELDS, AND SINCE THEN HAS LIVED IN HIDING ON THE MOORS IN A WOODEN CABIN. HE'S INNOCENT.
WHAT OF THIS JERGAN, COULD HE BE THE ONE RESPONSIBLE?
I HEAR A RUMOUR THAT YOU MIGHT BE ONE OF THE FINEST WRITTEN WE HAVE, FARDEN, WHERE WERE YOU WHEN THE BOOK WAS STOLEN?
I WAS IN NORTH ALBION, ON A MISSION GIVEN TO ME BY MY SUPERIOR. BUT PERHAPS, IF I MIGHT BE SO BOLD, LORD, IF YOU SUSPECT A TRAITOR, THEN SURELY THE MAGICK COUNCIL SHOULD BE CONSIDERED IN THIS INVESTIGATION.
NO ONE HERE IS BEING ACCUSED, FARDEN IS A LOYAL SERVANT AND HAS SERVED US WELL THROUGH THE YEARS, ARKMAGE HELYARD IS MERELY BEING WARY. I'M CURIOUS, WHY DID THEY FAIL IN SUMMONING THIS CREATURE?
JERGAN SAID THAT THE SPELL WOULD NEED ONE OF THE DARK ELVEN WELLS TO BRING THE CREATURE FROM THE OTHER SIDE, AND HE ALSO SEEMS TO THINK THERE MAY BE ONE IN EMANESKA THAT WE HAVE YET TO FIND..
AND I BELIEVE HIM.
DID HE DRAW YOU A MAP?!

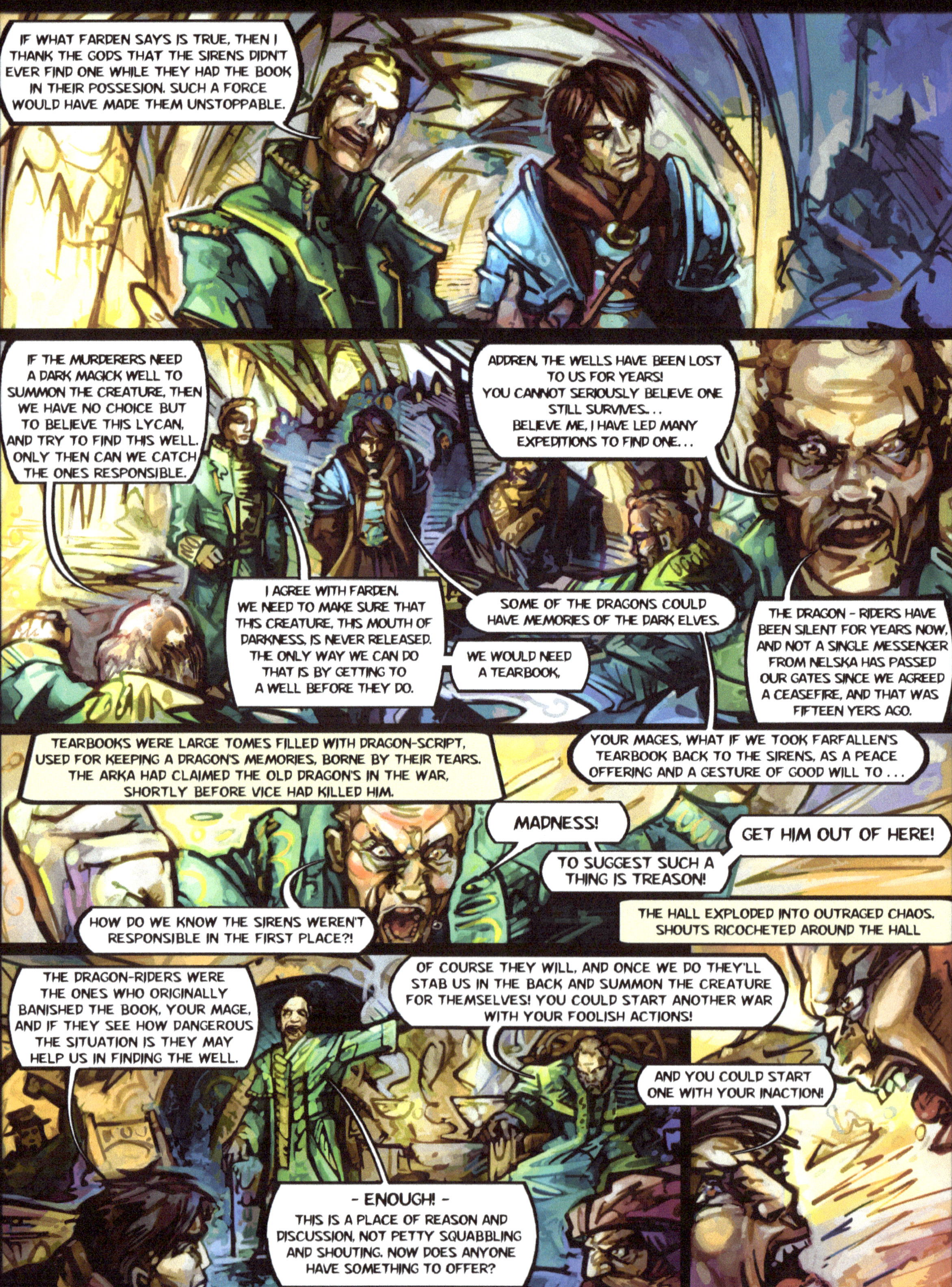

IF WHAT FARDEN SAYS IS TRUE, THEN I THANK THE GODS THAT THE SIRENS DIDN'T EVER FIND ONE WHILE THEY HAD THE BOOK IN THEIR POSSESION. SUCH A FORCE WOULD HAVE MADE THEM UNSTOPPABLE.
IF THE MURDERERS NEED A DARK MAGICK WELL TO SUMMON THE CREATURE, THEN WE HAVE NO CHOICE BUT TO BELIEVE THIS LYCAN, AND TRY TO FIND THIS WELL. ONLY THEN CAN WE CATCH THE ONES RESPONSIBLE.
ADDREN, THE WELLS HAVE BEEN LOST TO US FOR YEARS! YOU CANNOT SERIOUSLY BELIEVE ONE STILL SURVIVES... BELIEVE ME, I HAVE LED MANY EXPEDITIONS TO FIND ONE...
I AGREE WITH FARDEN. WE NEED TO MAKE SURE THAT THIS CREATURE, THIS MOUTH OF DARKNESS, IS NEVER RELEASED. THE ONLY WAY WE CAN DO THAT IS BY GETTING TO A WELL BEFORE THEY DO.
SOME OF THE DRAGONS COULD HAVE MEMORIES OF THE DARK ELVES.
WE WOULD NEED A TEARBOOK,
THE DRAGON - RIDERS HAVE BEEN SILENT FOR YEARS NOW, AND NOT A SINGLE MESSENGER FROM NELSKA HAS PASSED OUR GATES SINCE WE AGREED A CEASEFIRE, AND THAT WAS FIFTEEN YERS AGO.
TEARBOOKS WERE LARGE TOMES FILLED WITH DRAGON-SCRIPT, USED FOR KEEPING A DRAGON'S MEMORIES, BORNE BY THEIR TEARS. THE ARKA HAD CLAIMED THE OLD DRAGON'S IN THE WAR, SHORTLY BEFORE VICE HAD KILLED HIM.
YOUR MAGES, WHAT IF WE TOOK FARFALLEN'S TEARBOOK BACK TO THE SIRENS, AS A PEACE OFFERING AND A GESTURE OF GOOD WILL TO ...
MADNESS!
GET HIM OUT OF HERE!
TO SUGGEST SUCH A THING IS TREASON!
HOW DO WE KNOW THE SIRENS WEREN'T RESPONSIBLE IN THE FIRST PLACE?!
THE HALL EXPLODED INTO OUTRAGED CHAOS. SHOUTS RICOCHETED AROUND THE HALL
THE DRAGON-RIDERS WERE THE ONES WHO ORIGINALLY BANISHED THE BOOK, YOUR MAGE, AND IF THEY SEE HOW DANGEROUS THE SITUATION IS THEY MAY HELP US IN FINDING THE WELL.
OF COURSE THEY WILL, AND ONCE WE DO THEY'LL STAB US IN THE BACK AND SUMMON THE CREATURE FOR THEMSELVES! YOU COULD START ANOTHER WAR WITH YOUR FOOLISH ACTIONS!
AND YOU COULD START ONE WITH YOUR INACTION!
- ENOUGH! - THIS IS A PLACE OF REASON AND DISCUSSION, NOT PETTY SQUABBLING AND SHOUTING. NOW DOES ANYONE HAVE SOMETHING TO OFFER?

I SUGGEST THAT FARDEN SHOULD GO AS AN EMISSARY TO NELSKA, AND SPEAK WITH THE SIREN ELDERS. I WOULD RATHER GAIN THEIR HELP, THAN TRY TO FACE THIS THREAT ALONE. THIS CONCERNS ALL OF EMANESKA NOW, NOT JUST THE ARKA.
THEN IT IS DOWN TO A VOTE, HELYARD? CHOOSE YOUR SIDE.
VICE?
I SAY THAT THE DRAGON-RIDERS ARE THE ONES TO BLAME, AND WE'D BE FOOLISHLY THROWING EVERYTHING, AND I MEAN EVERYTHING, INTO THEIR CLAWS. I SAY NO.
ADDREN PAUSED FOR A MOMENT, AND EVERYBODY SEEMED TO HOLD THEIR BREATH...
THANK YOU, ARKMAGES, I WILL NOT FAIL YOU.
I SAY YES. FARDEN SHOULD TAKE THE TEARBOOK BACK TO NELSKA.
I SAY YES.
AND HERE ENTERED THE PROUD TRUMPETS. THE COUNCIL RUMBLED WITH MIXED OPINIONS AND A SCATTER OF APPLAUSE FROM ABOUT HALF OF THEM.
THANK YOU.
HELYARD WAS THE PICTURE OF RAGE, ARMS FOLDED, HE LANGUISHED IN HIS CHAIR LIKE A SPITEFUL LIZARD, STILL BORING INTO THE MAGE'S SKULL WITH HIS WOODEN EYES.

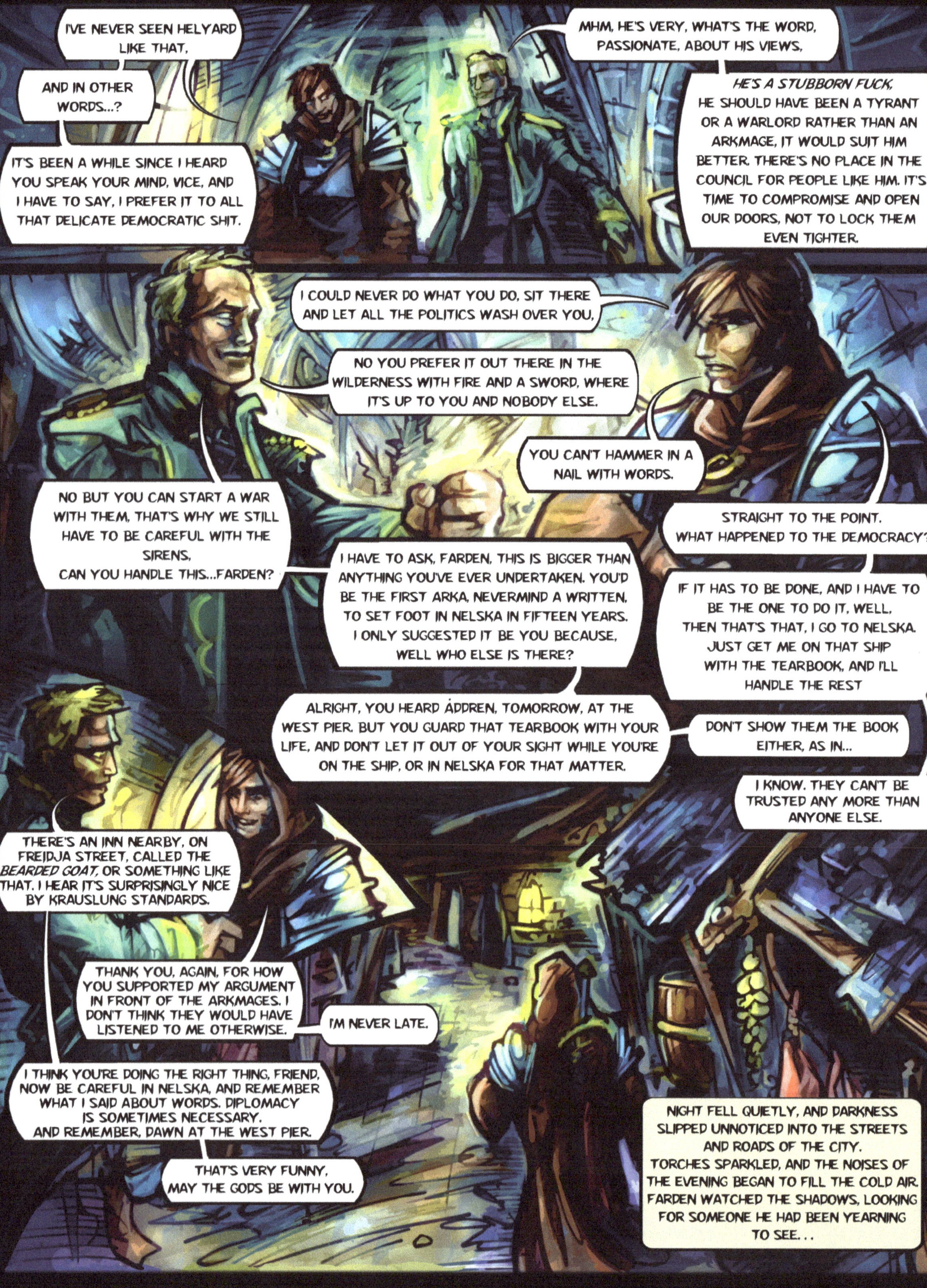

I'VE NEVER SEEN HELYARD LIKE THAT,
AND IN OTHER WORDS...?
IT'S BEEN A WHILE SINCE I HEARD YOU SPEAK YOUR MIND, VICE, AND I HAVE TO SAY, I PREFER IT TO ALL THAT DELICATE DEMOCRATIC SHIT.
MHM, HE'S VERY, WHAT'S THE WORD, PASSIONATE, ABOUT HIS VIEWS,
HE'S A STUBBORN FUCK, HE SHOULD HAVE BEEN A TYRANT OR A WARLORD RATHER THAN AN ARKMAGE, IT WOULD SUIT HIM BETTER. THERE'S NO PLACE IN THE COUNCIL FOR PEOPLE LIKE HIM. IT'S TIME TO COMPROMISE AND OPEN OUR DOORS, NOT TO LOCK THEM EVEN TIGHTER.
I COULD NEVER DO WHAT YOU DO, SIT THERE AND LET ALL THE POLITICS WASH OVER YOU,
NO YOU PREFER IT OUT THERE IN THE WILDERNESS WITH FIRE AND A SWORD, WHERE IT'S UP TO YOU AND NOBODY ELSE.
YOU CAN'T HAMMER IN A NAIL WITH WORDS.
STRAIGHT TO THE POINT. WHAT HAPPENED TO THE DEMOCRACY?
NO BUT YOU CAN START A WAR WITH THEM, THAT'S WHY WE STILL HAVE TO BE CAREFUL WITH THE SIRENS, CAN YOU HANDLE THIS...FARDEN?
I HAVE TO ASK, FARDEN, THIS IS BIGGER THAN ANYTHING YOU'VE EVER UNDERTAKEN. YOU'D BE THE FIRST ARKA, NEVERMIND A WRITTEN, TO SET FOOT IN NELSKA IN FIFTEEN YEARS. I ONLY SUGGESTED IT BE YOU BECAUSE, WELL WHO ELSE IS THERE?
IF IT HAS TO BE DONE, AND I HAVE TO BE THE ONE TO DO IT, WELL, THEN THAT'S THAT, I GO TO NELSKA. JUST GET ME ON THAT SHIP WITH THE TEARBOOK, AND I'LL HANDLE THE REST
ALRIGHT, YOU HEARD ÁDDREN, TOMORROW, AT THE WEST PIER. BUT YOU GUARD THAT TEARBOOK WITH YOUR LIFE, AND DON'T LET IT OUT OF YOUR SIGHT WHILE YOU'RE ON THE SHIP, OR IN NELSKA FOR THAT MATTER.
DON'T SHOW THEM THE BOOK EITHER, AS IN...
I KNOW. THEY CAN'T BE TRUSTED ANY MORE THAN ANYONE ELSE.
THERE'S AN INN NEARBY, ON FREIDJA STREET, CALLED THE BEARDED GOAT, OR SOMETHING LIKE THAT. I HEAR IT'S SURPRISINGLY NICE BY KRAUSLUNG STANDARDS.
THANK YOU, AGAIN, FOR HOW YOU SUPPORTED MY ARGUMENT IN FRONT OF THE ARKMAGES. I DON'T THINK THEY WOULD HAVE LISTENED TO ME OTHERWISE.
I'M NEVER LATE.
I THINK YOU'RE DOING THE RIGHT THING, FRIEND, NOW BE CAREFUL IN NELSKA, AND REMEMBER WHAT I SAID ABOUT WORDS. DIPLOMACY IS SOMETIMES NECESSARY. AND REMEMBER, DAWN AT THE WEST PIER.
THAT'S VERY FUNNY, MAY THE GODS BE WITH YOU.
NIGHT FELL QUIETLY, AND DARKNESS SLIPPED UNNOTICED INTO THE STREETS AND ROADS OF THE CITY. TORCHES SPARKLED, AND THE NOISES OF THE EVENING BEGAN TO FILL THE COLD AIR. FARDEN WATCHED THE SHADOWS, LOOKING FOR SOMEONE HE HAD BEEN YEARNING TO SEE...

TWO FIGURES WALKED SILENTLY THROUGH AN ALLEYWAY, CLOAKED AND HOODED, NEAR TO WHERE THE MAIN WALL MET THE MOUNTAIN ROCK. AS THEY WANDERED FURTHER AND FURTHER AWAY FROM PRYING EYES, HANDS REACHED OUT TO TORCHES AND THEY HISSED AND DIED ONE BY ONE. THE SHADOWS WERE AS THICK AS BLACK VELVET, AND THE TWO STRANGERS KNEW IT.
HOW LONG ARE YOU STAYING FOR?
THEY'RE SENDING ME AWAY AGAIN, TOMORROW.
I TOLD YOU I'D FIND YOU.
WHY'S IT SO DAAAAARK? (SINGING)
I'M GLAD YOU DID.
I JUST WANT TO SPEND MORE THAN TWO MINUTES WITH YOU BEFORE YOU DISAPPEAR AGAIN.
I KNOW IT'S DANGEROUS FOR US, AND NOW THAT THERE'S THE RITUAL... IT'LL BE AGAINST THE LAW
WHOAAA! HIDIN' IN THE SHADOWS ARE WE?
I KNOW. BUT I DON'T CARE, I WANT YOU.
QUIET YOURSELF, FOOL, BEFORE I DO IT FOR YOU.
SO DO I.
DON'T, FARDEN.
YOU'VE ALWAYS BEEN SO QUICK TO ANGER, FARDEN.
KEEP MOVING.
WHO'S YOUR PRETTY FRIEND MATE? SHE CAN COME HOME WITH ME IF YE LIKE?
I DON'T LIKE PEOPLE.
BUT YOU LIKE ME.
GODS, FARDEN, YOU HAVE TO STOP WORRYING ABOUT THIS RITUAL. I'M READY FOR THIS.
YOU'RE DIFFERENT, YOU'RE NOT LIKE THE OTHERS. SOMEHOW YOU CAN KEEP ME CALM. WELL, UP UNTIL NOW.
THE MAN LEFT, HOLLERING AND HOOTING WITH EVERY STEP.
DO YOU BLAME ME?
NO, BUT WE CAN DEAL WITH THIS WHEN YOU GET BACK. NOT NOW. I THINK IT'S TIME I LEFT. PLEASE BE SAFE, WHEREVER YOU'RE GOING.
SHE RAN A HAND OVER HIS WEATHERED FACE, AND THEN LEFT, MELTING INTO THE DARKNESS. FARDEN STAYED A WHILE, WAITING UNTIL IT WAS SAFE, AND THEN WALKED OFF IN A DIFFERENT DIRECTION.

FARDEN WANDERED SLOWLY DOWN FREIDJA STREET, DRIFTING THROUGH THE NIGHTTIME SOUNDS OF THE CITY.
THE STREET WAS CHOKED WITH DRUNKEN PEOPLE AND BEADY-EYED STRANGERS. FARDEN KEPT HIS HOOD LOW AND HIS PACE BRISK. HE HEARD THE CLATTER OF THE BEARDED GOAT BEFORE HE SAW IT. HE PAUSED AT ITS DOOR BEFORE ENTERING.
THE INN WAS LOUD AND FULL OF DRUNKEN FOOLS. A SKALD WAS REGALING THE RUMBUSTIOUS CROWD WITH STORIES ABOUT THE FAERIE INCIDENT. HE STOOD ON A TABLE NEAR THE DOOR PLAYING HIS STRINGED LJOT, KICKING TANKARDS OF BEER WITH HIS MUDDY FEET, AND BELTING OUT THE WORDS AT THE TOP OF HIS VOICE. A FEW WOMEN IN THIN FRILLY DRESSES LOUNGED ABOUT THE PLACE, GRINNING AT ANY MAN WHO CAME CLOSE AND BECKONING THEM CLOSER WITH CROOKED FINGERS, NAILS PAINTED WITH GAUDY YELLOWS AND REDS. THE MEN CHEERED AND CLANGED THEIR TANKARDS TOGETHER, SINGING ALONG, SWINGING SOME OF THE MORE SOBER WOMEN AROUND IN DRUNKEN JIGS. THE MAGE WATCHED THEM IMPASSIVELY. ALCOHOL WORKED IN MYSTERIOUS WAYS.

FARDEN FOUND A QUIET CORNER BY THE FIREPLACE IN THE DIM RECESSES OF THE INN. FARDEN LOOKED INTO THE CRACKLING FLAMES AND SWIRLED HIS SWEET RED WINE AROUND IN THE WOODEN CUP, THINKING ABOUT HIS DAY, AND TRYING NOT TO THINK ABOUT CHESKA. THE FIRE WAS WARMING HIS COLD TOES EVEN THROUGH HIS THICK TRAVELLING BOOTS, AND THE WARMTH AND THE WINE WERE STARTING TO MAKE HIM SLEEPY.
JORG
NEXT TO HIM, NEARER TO THE WALL IN A SHADOWY CORNER, WAS AN OLD DIRTY BEGGAR SMOKING A LONG DIRTY PIPE. FARDEN HAD SEEN HIM EARLIER, SNORING AWAY TO HIMSELF NEAR THE WARMTH OF THE FIRE, BUT NOW HE WAS AWAKE AND PEERING ABOUT THE PLACE WITH HIS BEADY RAT-EYES.
WHAT DO YOU WANT?
OH NOTHIN', THOUGHT I'D LOOK AT YER, SEEIN' AS YEWS LOOKIN' AT ME.
YEW LOOK LIKE A STRONG FELLOW THOUGH, DON'T YER? ALL QUIET AND SAD ON YER OWN,
WHAT'S IT TO YOU?
OH NOTHIN' AT ALL, FRIEND, JUS' MAKIN' CONVERSATION S'ALL,
WELL I'D APPRECIATE THE PEACE AND QUIET IF IT'S ALL THE SAME TO YOU.
YEW THAT MAGE? THE ONE I 'EARD ABOUT?
THERE ARE A LOT OF MAGES IN KRAUSLUNG OLD MAN, I'M NOT ONE OF THEM.
DON'T CALL ME THAT. FINE, I'M IN NUMBER SIXTEEN, IF YOU CAN COUNT THAT HIGH, THE ONE WITH THE RED DOOR.
HEEHEE, FAIR ENOUGH,, BUT I SEEN YEW AROUND, MAGE, RUNNIN' HERE, RUNNIN' THERE, YER IMPORTANT THEY SAY, ONE OF THE OLDER ONES. I 'EARD ABOUT YEW AN THOSE MINOTAURS SEV'RAL YEARS BACK?
I DON'T SMOKE.
SAID YEW ALMOST TOOK 'EM ALL SINGLE 'ANDED. SAW YER AT THE ARKATHEDRAL TOO, AN' I CAN SPOT THOSE PRETTY VAMBRACES A MILE AWAY, FANCY A BIT?
WASN'T TALKIN' 'BOUT TABACCY NOW WAS I...?
HOW MUCH?
SOMETIMES AN OLD MAN JUS' LIKES A BODY TO SMOKE WITH, MAKES A CHANGE DON'T IT, MAGE?

FARDEN SWEPT UP THE NEARBY STAIRCASE AND DISAPPEARED INTO THE SHADOWS OF THE CORRIDOR. AFTER FINDING HIS ROOM IN THE GLOOMY HALLWAY HE OPENED THE DOOR AND LIT THE FIREPLACE WITH A QUICK SPELL.
HE IMPATIENTLY PLAYED WITH FLASHING SPARKS ON HIS PALM. UNWELCOME THOUGHTS GATHERED, MEMORIES AND DEAD FACES LAUGHED AT HIM. CHESKA HOVERED IN HIS MIND, PALE, AND STILL. HE WANTED TO STOP THINKING.
KNOCK KNOCK
A SHORT WHILE PASSED AND THEN THERE CAME A BONY KNOCK ON THE WOODEN DOOR.
GIVE ME A MOMENT.
HAVE A SEAT.
WHAT'S THAT?
GIM, SKIFF, REDRAW, BLAGG, NEVERMAR, YOU ALWAYS SMOKE IT IN A PIPE,
IF I FIND OUT THAT YOU'VE TOLD ANYONE, ANYONE ABOUT THIS, THEN I WILL FIND YOU, OLD MAN, AND I WILL KILL YOU. UNDERSTAND?
DON'T CALL ME THAT.
IT'S HARSH.
DON'T KNOW NO ONE TO TELL, MAGE, YEW CAN TRUST ME
TASTES GOOD DON'T IT,

HE TOOK ANOTHER PAINFUL DRAG AND TRIED TO RELAX IN HIS CHAIR, FEELING A SLIGHT HEADINESS TINGLING ALL THROUGHOUT HIS SKULL.
HE OFFERED THE PIPE BACK TO THE OLD MAN AND HE GRABBED AT IT WITH GRUBBY FINGERS. AFTER A FEW QUICK PUFFS HE PASSED IT BACK TO FARDEN WITH ANOTHER KNOWING GRIN.
THE MAN WATCHED FARDEN SMOKE THE PIPE WITH A HUNGRY EXPRESSION, BUT FARDEN DIDN'T EVEN NOTICE.
HE HELD THE SMOKE IN HIS CHEST AND FELT THE BACK OF HIS EYES SHIVER AND HIS TEMPLES QUIVER. HIS ARMS FELT A HUNDRED FEET LONG AND HIS FINGERS MOVED THROUGH SICKLY HONEY.
THE OLD TRAMP SHOOK AND BOUNCED, AND HIS JITTERY BED SHIFTED AROUND IN AN IMAGINARY EARTHQUAKE, SMOKE FILLED HIS EYES. LUNGS BURNT. AN INTENSE FEELING OF DIZZINESS POUNDED AGAINST THE INSIDE OF FARDEN'S SKULL.
HE CLOSED HIS EYES TO WATCH COLOURS COLLIDE, AND OPENED THEM TO FIND HE WAS SUDDENLY ALONE. THE OLD BEGGAR WAS LONG GONE. A PILLOW HIJACKED HIS HEAD AND HE DRIFTED OFF INTO A HEAVY, DRUG-LADEN SLEEP.
GODS DANCED AROUND HIS ROOM, AND DAEMONS WATCHED FROM THE CORNERS AND RAFTERS, QUOTING SOMETHING ABOUT BLOOD AND HISTORY. DARKNESS TOOK HIM.

FARDEN WAS DREAMING AGAIN. HE STOOD IN THE SHADOW OF A BLACK MOUNTAIN.
THE WIND WHISTLED THROUGH THE ROCKS, MAKING AN EERIE SOUND LIKE A FARAWAY HORN CRYING FOR HELP, OR A WOUNDED ANIMAL WAILING AWAY ITS LAST FEW HOURS.
THE MAGE LOOKED BEHIND HIM AND SAW RAZOR-SHARP CRAGS OF ROCK HANGING OVER HIM, A BARE, FACELESS CLIFF OF JET AND OBSIDIAN COMING STRAIGHT OUT OF THE SAND AND TOWERING INTO THE SKY.
FARDEN LOOKED UP AT THE SKY, THAT PURE EMPTY SKY, AND FELT A TRANQUILITY HE HAD NEVER FELT BEFORE SUDDENLY WASH OVER HIM.
A BLACK SHAPE FLUTTERED IN HIS PERIPHERAL VISION, AND FARDEN TURNED HIS HEAD. A CROW, OR A RAVEN, SOME SORT OF BLACK BIRD, FLAPPED AIMLESSLY AROUND THE ROCKY LEDGES OF THE BLACK CLIFF.
DESPERATELY, THE BIRD TRIED TO FIND A SAFE PLACE BETWEEN THE ROCKS.
THE BIRD WAS TRYING TO STAY OUT OF REACH OF A SKINNY BLACK CAT THAT DANCED BELOW IT ON ITS HINDLEGS. THE BIRD DITHERED IN MIDAIR, NARROWLY AVOIDING THE CLAWING SWIPES OF THE MANGY CAT.
THE CAT CROUCHED AND WATCHED ITS PREY. FARDEN TRIED TO SHOUT AND SCARE EITHER OF THE ANIMALS AWAY, BUT THE HOT WIND SNATCHED THE WORDS FROM HIS LIPS, AND HE YELLED IN COMPLETE SILENCE.

UNTIL SUDDENLY, CHOOSING ITS PERFECT MOMENT, THE CAT SHOT INTO THE AIR AND DRAGGED THE BIRD TO THE SAND.
THE CAT HUNKERED DOWN AND ITS HAUNCHES TWITCHED AND WIGGLED.
THE THING FLAPPED AND CRIED, BUT THE CAT WAS MERCILESS.
FARDEN LOOKED AT THE CAT, AND SAW HER STARING BACK AT HIM WITH THOSE OBSIDIAN EYES. BLOOD DRIPPED FROM HER FANGS.
THE SAND HAD BECOME A RED POOL. THE CAT TOOK A SLOW STEP FORWARD TOWARDS HIM.
YOU'RE BETWEEN A ROCK AND A HARD PLACE... SO TO SPEAK, THEY'VE GOT YOU ALL IN A FLAP.
AN ECHOING VOICE SPOKE IN THE BACK OF HIS HEAD. FARDEN TRIED TO ANSWER, BUT NO SOUND CAME FROM HIS MOUTH. THE CAT CONTINUED TO MOVE FORWARD. BLACK SHAPES AND BEADY EYES HID BEHIND THE CRAGS AND WATCHED HIM.
IT'S YOU THEY WANT, JUST AS THEY ONCE WANTED ME.
A TALON SLICED ACROSS HIS BACK,
CLAWS RIPPED FLESH FROM BONE.
A BEAK TORE A HOLE IN HIS SIDE,
. . .FOLLOW THE DRAGONS.

NO MORE THAN A HANDFUL OF HOURS AFTER HE HAD COLLAPSED INTO HIS BED, THE FIRST STREAKS OF DAWN STARTED TO STRETCH ACROSS THE DIM SKY, AND FARDEN AWOKE WITH A POUNDING HEADACHE.
HE TRIED TO CAST A SMALL HEALING SPELL AND THE MAGICK SMASHED AGAINST HIS SKULL LIKE A SLEDGEHAMMER.
STOICALLY, HE HAULED HIS SWORD OVER HIS BACK, WINCING, HE FASTENED HIS CLOAK AROUND HIM AND SLAMMED THE DOOR MUCH TO THE DISMAY OF HIS HEAD.
HE FELL OUT OF BED AND COLLIDED WITH THE COLD WOODEN FLOOR WITH A GROAN.
FARDEN SHOOK HIS HEAD GINGERLY, AND TRIED TO FORGET THE STRANGE NIGHTMARE.
THE STREETS OF KRAUSLUNG WERE GLOOMY IN THE EARLY DAWN LIGHT,
THE SHADOWY CLOUDS HUNG LIKE A BLANKET OVER THE MOUNTAINS AND THE SLUMBERING CITY BY THE SEA.
SPARE A COIN SIR?
GODS BE WITH YOU SIRE!
PEOPLE WERE NOW BEGINNING TO FILL THE THOROUGHFARE, LAUGHING AND TALKING LOUDLY DESPITE THE EARLY MORNING.
FARDEN WATCHED AN ATTRACTIVE PEASANT GIRL LEAVE A RICH-LOOKING HOUSE AND SKIP DOWN THE STREET WITH A COY LITTLE SMILE. STILL DOING UP HER BLOUSE AND WIPING SMUDGED MAKEUP FROM HER FACE WHEN SHE DISAPPEARED AROUND A CORNER.
A SHORT BEARDED MAN, WHO SEEMED TO STILL BE DRUNK FROM THE NIGHT BEFORE, SHOUTED IMPATIENTLY AT THE CLOSED DOORS OF A BAKERY WHILE CLINGING TO A LAMP POST TO KEEP FROM FALLING OVER
SUCH WAS THE WAY OF KRAUSLUNG SOCIETY.

HE WALKED FOR ANOTHER HALF AN HOUR BEFORE HE CAME TO A SHORT BALCONY THAT OVERLOOKED A SQUARE AND THE WEST CURVE OF PORT RÓS.
THE MAGE STOOD AGAINST THE STONE RAILINGS AND SNIFFED THE SALTY AIR, FEELING THE FRESH BREEZE TRY TO WORK ITS CHARM ON HIS HEADACHE.
A COLD MIST HAD CREPT ACROSS THE SEA IN THE NIGHT, AND NOW IT LINGERED IN THICK WISPS AND TRAILS AT THE EDGES OF THE HARBOUR WALLS. THE SHIPS IN THEIR DOCKS ROLLED GENTLY ON THE CALM BLUE-GREEN SWELL, CROWDED SIDE-BY-SIDE AND TETHERED BY THICK ROPES.
STALLS HAD STARTED SERVING FRIED MEAT AND BREAD, BOILING CHEAP MOSS TEA FOR THE SLEEPY SAILORS. THE SMELLS OF FARSKA AND FISH SOUP AND THE INFAMOUS SEA-SERPENT PIE, WERE THICK IN THE COLD AIR.
FARDEN WAITED IN LINE AT A STALL AND GRABBED A QUICK BREAD ROLL STUFFED WITH CHEAP GREASY VENISON.
FARDEN !
THE MAGE WALKED FURTHER ALONG THE WOODEN JETTY TOWARDS THE WEST PIER.
HE BIT INTO IT RAVENOUSLY AND TRIED TO CHEW IN A WAY THAT DIDN'T CAUSE SPARKS TO FLY BEHIND HIS EYES. THE FOOD TASTED LIKE ASH IN HIS MOUTH. A SWIG OF BRACKISH TEA JUST REMINDED HIM OF THE HERBY CHARCOAL TASTE OF THE NEVERMAR.
HE LOOKED AHEAD AND SPIED A SHIP FLYING THE GOLDEN SCALES OF THE ARKA. HE HEADED OFF IN ITS GENERAL DIRECTION. FARDEN WAS SLOWLY REALISING HOW MUCH HE WAS DREADING THE SHIP, AND THE TURBULENT, CHURNING JOURNEY THAT WAS WAITING FOR HIM.

HIS OWN NAME SURPRISED HIM AND HE TURNED TO SEE ADDREN AND HELYARD FLANKED BY A DOZEN OR SO ARMOURED SOLDIERS.
I TRUST YOU SLEPT WELL, FARDEN?
I RESTED WELL, YOUR MAGE, THANK YOU.
GOOD, WE NEED YOU VIGILANT AND WELL PREPARED FOR THIS TRIP. I HAVE CONVINCED HELYARD TO PROVIDE YOU WITH FAIR WEATHER FOR AS FAR AS HE CAN MANAGE.
HELYARD JUST GRUNTED. FARDEN HAD HEARD THE RUMOURS ABOUT THE ARKMAGE'S POWER OVER THE LOCAL WEATHER, AND IT HAD BEEN KNOWN, THAT ON OCCASION, SUMMER DAYS WOULD BE SURPRISED WITH FREAK SNOW. THAT HAD BEEN BEFORE THE DAYS OF THE LONG WINTER.
MEANWHILE, A HAWK HAS BEEN SENT TO NELSKA AND THE CITADEL OF HJAUSSFEN TO WARN THEM OF AN EMISSARY FROM THE ARKA. I DID NOT MENTION THE TRUE INTENTION OF YOUR MISSION IN THE LETTER.
MAKE SURE YOU READ IT FIRST, MAGE, AND WITH THE DRAGON-RIDERS. MOST IMPORTANTLY DON'T LET THEM HOLD INFORMATION FROM YOU, AND DON'T YOU DARE JEOPARDISE THIS CEASEFIRE.
HERE IS THE TEARBOOK. KEEP IT SAFE AT ALL TIMES. THESE SAILORS ARE LOYAL, AS ARE THE SOLDIERS, BUT GREED MAY CHANGE THEIR MINDS.
THE SHIP WAS A LOW CARRACK, A DARK MAHOGANY BROWN IN COLOUR, WITH TALL DECKS AND PINE RAILS.
FARDEN MARVELLED AT THE LENGTHS OF ROPE THAT SEEMED TO HOLD THE FAT SHIP TOGETHER, WRAPPED AROUND ITS STOUT RIGGING AND SAILS LIKE A SPIDER'S WEB ON A HEDGE.
BARNACLES AND GREEN ALGAE FESTOONED THE BATTERED HULL, AND A SAD LOOKING UNICORN THAT HAD SEEN BETTER DAYS WAS THE FIGUREHEAD.

ADDREN WELCOMED A GRIZZLY OLD MAN TO THEIR PARTY. HE LOOKED AS THOUGH HE HAD BEEN BORN AT SEA.
THE SARUNN IS A GOOD SHIP, WE SHOULD BE THERE IN ABOUT FIVE OR SIX DAYS, TRAVELLING 'ROUND THE COAST,
EXCELLENT. THANK YOU, CAPTAIN
FARDEN, THIS IS CAPTAIN HEOLD.
GOOD TO MEET YER FARDEN,
FARDEN, I HONESTLY WISH I DIDN'T HAVE TO ASK YOU TO CARRY OUT THIS MISSION, BUT IF I THOUGHT THAT A MAN BETTER SUITED TO THE TASK EXISTED, I WOULD ASK HIM.
THANK YOU, YOUR MAGE.
I KNOW HOW IMPORTANT THIS IS FOR OUR PEOPLE, ARKMAGE, AND TRUST ME THERE IS NO MEASURE I WON'T TAKE.
AND YOU MAY THINK THAT HELYARD AND THE REST OF THE COUNCIL ARE AGAINST YOU IN THIS, BUT BELIEVE ME YOU ARE DOING THE RIGHT THING. NOT ONLY COULD WE HAVE A CHANCE TO STOP THIS MALICIOUS PLOT IN ITS TRACKS, BUT WE COULD FINALLY HAVE A CHANCE OF PEACE WITH THE DRAGON-RIDERS.
RIGHT, LET'S STEP TO IT LIVELY, LADS, PREPARE TO CAST OFF AS SOON AS WE CAN!
JUST...BE CAREFUL, MAGE. WE MUST PRAY TO THE GODS, AND WAIT FOR YOUR MESSAGE,
LET'S HOPE THEN, THAT OUR GODS ARE STRONGER THAN OUR ENEMY'S.
HOPE, THERE WILL BE, WRITTEN, FOR THE GODS AND FOR YOU. MAY NJORD PROTECT YOU.
A FEW NEARBY SAILORS RUMBLED IN AGREEMENT, THOUGH THEY EYED FARDEN LIKE HE CARRIED THE PLAGUE.
THE MAGE SIGHED INWARDLY, NODDED HIS THANKS TO HIS SUPERIOR, BOWED, AND THEN CLIMBED THE RAMP UP TO THE SHIP. THE THREE OR FOUR ARKA SOLDIERS HAD FOUND THEIR BERTHS IN THE UNDER DECKS, AND THE MAGE DECIDED TO GO DO THE SAME. WITH ONE LAST WAVE TO THE ARKMAGES AND THEIR ENTOURAGE HE DUCKED UNDER A HATCH AND WENT BELOW.

FARDEN QUICKLY WENT TO THE CORNER OF HIS CABIN AND THREW HIS GUTS UP IN THE WOODEN PAIL. HIS HEAD LURCHED WITH HIS STOMACH AND THE WORLD BURST INTO SPARKS AND LEAPS.
FARDEN CURSED AND SLUMPED BACK AGAINST THE BOLTED-DOWN BED, WIPING THE MESS FROM HIS CHIN. HE KNEW BETTER BUT HAD TO TRY A SPELL ON THE OFF-CHANCE THE NEVERMAR HAD WORN OFF BUT NO MAGICK CAME. ONLY PAIN. IF THIS LASTED LONGER THAN FIVE OR SIX DAYS HE WAS IN TROUBLE.. HE HAD NEVER FELT THIS POWERLESS BEFORE. HE JUST LAY THERE, BREATHING.
AFTER A WHILE, FARDEN FELT THE SHIP DRIFT FREE OF THE DOCK AND THE WAVES BENEATH THEM MADE THE SHIP ROCK BACK AND FORTH.
THE MAGE FOUGHT BACK BILE AND A POUNDING HEADACHE WHILE THE SAILORS ABOVE HIM SENT THE SHIP LEANING INTO THE GROWING WIND.
THE SARUNN CLEARED THE BOARDWALK AND SAILED OUT INTO THE MOUTH OF THE PORT.

THE FIRST FEW DAYS WERE UNEVENTFUL. FARDEN HID IN HIS ROOM, FEELING EVERY PITCH AND ROLL OF THE VESSEL IN HIS UNCOMFORTABLE WOODEN BED. AS THEY ROUNDED THE COASTLINE TO HEAD TOWARDS THE JÖRMUNN SEA, PAST THE CLIFFS OF HALORN, THE CLOUDS STARTED TO PILE UP AND DARKEN, BRINGING SQUALLS AND BITTER GALES TO HAMMER DOWN ON THE SHIP.
ON THE FIRST DAY, A SMALL BLACK CAT FOUND ITS WAY INTO THE ROOM. FARDEN ASSUMED IT WAS THE SHIP'S CAT. A LITTLE GOOD LUCK CHARM AGAINST BAD WEATHER.
THE MAGE SPENT HIS TIME MEDITATING AND TRYING TO GET HIS POWER BACK, OR ABSENTLY MAPPING THE STARS WHEN THE DECK WAS QUIET ENOUGH. FARDEN FOUND HIMSELF LYING AWAKE ON THE COLD NIGHTS, PICTURING CHESKA'S BEAUTIFUL EYES IN HIS TIRED MIND AND THINKING LONG AND HARD ABOUT THINGS LIKE HER BODY, HER LAUGH AND A HUNDRED OTHER THINGS, NOT TO MENTION THEIR FUTURE.
FARDEN HAD FINALLY RID HIMSELF OF HIS HEADACHE AND THE BUCKET HAD NOT BEEN TOUCHED IN ALMOST A DAY NOW.
HIS MAGICK, HOWEVER, HAD NOT RETURNED IN THE SLIGHTEST.
ONCE ON THE SECOND DAY, OUT OF PURE BOREDOM AND CURIOSITY, HE TOOK THE TEARBOOK FROM ITS SATCHEL AND IDLY FLIPPED THROUGH ITS PAGES. THEY WERE UTTERLY BLANK. NOT A SINGLE MARK COULD BE FOUND ANYWHERE. FARDEN HAD BEEN RATHER DISAPPOINTED.
FARDEN WALKED ALONG THE DECKS AT DAWN, ACCOMPANIED BY THE LITHE BLACK CAT. TIME FELT LIKE TREACLE ON THE SHIP AND FARDEN DREADED THE CONSTANT WARY LOOKS FROM THE SUPERSTITIOUS SAILORS.
A MAN STOOD ON WATCH TO FARDEN'S RIGHT. HE WAS A THIN WIRY MAN AND LOOKED STRONG DESPITE HIS SIZE.
LOOKS FAIRLY BAD, I AGREE. CAP'N SHOULD RIDE 'ER WELL.
YOU HAVE A FINE CAPTAIN, IT SEEMS.
MORNIN' MATE
KARGA'S THE NAME.
FARDEN, MORNING. WEATHER LOOKS BAD
I WOULDN'T REALLY KNOW. HE SEEMS A FINE FELLOW, BUT I'M JUS' A STAND-IN FOR THIS VOYAGE. OTHER MAN GOT SICK. . . PLAGUE PROBABLY.
OI MATE, LOOK AT THIS, STORM GIANTS!

BETWEEN A GAP IN THE IMMENSE STORM-FRONT, TENDRILS OF CLOUD BEGAN TO FORM TWO SHAPES THAT TOWERED ABOVE THE SEAS. THEY REARED OUT OF THE CLOUDS AND STOOD UPRIGHT TO FACE EACH OTHER, LOOKING FOR ALL THE WORLD LIKE TWO BRAWNY MEN CARVED FROM CLOUD, AND THEY BEGAN TO MOVE. THUNDER RUMBLED, AND FARDEN MOVED CLOSER TO THE RAILING TO STARE IN AMAZEMENT AS THE GIANTS LUNGED AT EACH OTHER AND THREW PUNCH AFTER PUNCH UNTIL THE SKY SHOOK.
WHAT IN GODS' NAME IS GOIN' ON?!
STORM GIANTS CAP'N!
BUT AS QUICKLY AS THEY HAD APPEARED THEY VANISHED AND AFTER A FEW MORE THUNDER CLAPS THE GIANTS MELTED BACK INTO THE CLOUDS.
DESPITE THE ROCKING OF THE SHIP AND THE BAD WEATHER, THE MAGE FELL INTO A DEEP SLEEP UNTIL LATER THE NEXT DAY. AS HE ROLLED OUT OF HIS BED, HE IDLY WONDERED WHAT THE COUNCIL WOULD THINK OF HIM USING THE TEARBOOK AS A PILLOW. HE RUBBED HIS EYES, YAWNED, AND HEADED TOWARDS THE GALLEY.
ALRIGHT THERE, SIR?
FINE, THANKS, I WAS JUST WONDERING IF THERE'S ANY LUNCH LEFT OVER? I SEEMED TO HAVE MISSED IT.
ONCE HE WAS SATISFIED, FARDEN PATTED HIS BELLY. HE SUDDENLY REALISED THAT HE HAD LEFT THE TEARBOOK ON HIS BED IN HIS ROOM. A COLD CHILL SHIVERED THROUGH HIM, AND HE BEGAN TO BACK OUT OF THE GALLEY.
'FARSKAS' IN THE PAN, OR THERE'S SOME SHARK 'ERE THAT THE FIRST MATE CAUGHT,
THERE'LL BE SUMMIN' NEW TOMORROW AS WELL.
THE SMELL OF THE CHEAP FISHY STEW FILLED FARDEN WITH RAVENOUS HUNGER. HE DUG IN WITH A WOODEN SPOON THAT DIDN'T LOOK TOO CLEAN. BUT THE MAGE WAS TOO HUNGRY TO CARE. HE DUG IN EAGERLY.

THE MAGE PIVOTED ON HIS HEEL AND SPRINTED DOWN THE CORRIDOR.
HE MADE HIS WAY BELOW AND PUSHED THE DOOR TO HIS CABIN OPEN WITH A BANG.
WHAT THE FUCK ARE YOU DOING?
KARGA WAS HUNCHED OVER THE BED, FLICKING LAZILY THROUGH THE PAGES OF THE TEARBOOK.
WHATEVER YOU SAY, FARDEN.
I KNEW YOU WOULDN'T LEAVE IT FOR LONG.
GET AWAY FROM THE BOOK.
HE WAS RIGHT, IT IS EMPTY.
WHATEVER YOU SAY. . . YOU HAVE NO IDEA WHAT'S GOING ON, DO YOU?
WHAT ARE YOU DOING WITH MY BOOK?
WIPE THAT SMILE OFF YOUR FACE OR I'LL THROW YOU OVERBOARD!
I'D LIKE TO SEE YOU TRY.
I THINK WE SHOULD SEE WHAT HEOLD HAS TO SAY ABOUT ALL THIS,
MOVE, GET OUT!

RED MAGMA BURST FROM KARGA'S FINGERTIPS AND A SEARING PYROCLASTIC CLOUD OF FIRE HIT THE MAGE IN THE CHEST. IT KNOCKED HIM STRAIGHT THROUGH THE WALL OF THE CABIN. HE SWUNG HIS SWORD BLIINDLY IN THE BURNING SMOG.
FARDEN WAITED AND SLOWED HIS BREATH, CONCENTRATING HARD ON NOT CHOKING. HE LISTENED INTENTLY FOR THE RIGHT MOMENT TO POUNCE.
COME OUT HERE AND FIGHT!
I'M RIGHT HERE, KARGA, COME AND FIND ME!
BUT KARGA SPUN AROUND AND HELD HIS HANDS UP TO BLOCK THE SWING. JUST BEFORE THE BLADE CARVED THROUGH HIS FINGERS, A PULSE OF ENERGY EXPLODED FROM HIS PALMS AND THE SWORD REBOUNDED WITH A CLANG. FARDEN SWUNG AGAIN AND THRUST DEADLY STEEL INTO THE MAN'S FACE. BUT AGAIN KARGA BLOCKED. THE SWORD WHINED AND BOUNCED AWAY.
WITH A YELL, HE JUMPED UP AND SWUNG HIS SWORD AT HIS ASSAILANT'S HEAD.
KARGA SNEERED, AND HIS EYES FLASHED A DEEP RED. THIS MAN HAD DARK MAGICK IN HIM, THOUGHT FARDEN, A SERVANT OF THE FORBIDDEN.
CRUNCH
WHO ARE YOU?
THE MAN WHO WAS SENT TO KILL YOU!
SEIZING HIS CHANCE, FARDEN TOOK A STEP FORWARD AND SLAMMED HIS FOREHEAD INTO KARGA'S NOSE.
YOU CAN'T FIGHT ME WITH MAGICK, FARDEN? WHAT'S WRONG? I WAS TOLD YOU'D BE FUN! A FAIR MATCH FOR A SORCERER OF MY STRENGTH.

KARGA CLENCHED HIS FIST AND SHOUTED FOREIGN WORDS. ALL OF A SUDDEN THE SHADOWS IN THE DIM UNDERBELLY OF THE SHIP CAME ALIVE AND GRABBED AT THE MAGE.
FARDEN DODGED UNDER BEAMS AND ROPES AND GRABBED THE STURDY WOODEN RAIL OF THE LADDER.
FIGHT ME!
BAA!
WHAT'S GOIN' ON ' ERE?!
FARDEN PUSHED THE HATCH ABOVE HIM AND LUCKILY IT CAME FREE. HE QUICKLY RAN UP THE LADDER AND SKIDDED ONTO THE DECK.
IT'S ONE OF YOUR CREW, KARGA! HE'S BEEN SENT TO RUIN THIS MISSION.
FARDEN TOOK COVER BEHIND A CRATE. SOMETHING STIRRED IN HIS SPINE, A TINGLING ACROSS HIS BROAD SHOULDERS THAT HE KNEW VERY WELL INDEED. THANK THE GODS.
YOU WANT TO SEE SOME MAGICK?
COME OUT, COWARD! YOU SHOULD KNOW BETTER THAN TO INTERFERE WITH THE POWER OF THE ELVES.
AS THE DECK BENEATH HIS FEET BEGAN TO RATTLE AND CRACK, TIME CAUGHT UP WITH ITSELF WITH A THUNDERCLAP. AT THE WHEEL, HEOLD'S FACE DRAINED OF COLOUR AND HIS SHOUT CHILLED EVERYBODY ON DECK.
FARDEN LIFTED HIS ARMS THROUGH THE THE SLOWING RAIN, SINGLE DROPLETS SLIDING OVER HIS HANDS LIKE CLEAR MERCURY. THE AIR AROUND HIM BUZZED WITH MAGICK. HE COULD FEEL HIS TATTOOS BURNING WHITE HOT. HIS HANDS SHOOK, AND FOR THE BRIEFEST OF MOMENTS, TIME STOPPED AND THE STORMY WORLD AROUND HIM BECAME QUIET.
WAVE

WITH A BLINDING FLASH, A SEARING TOWER OF FIRE ERUPTED FROM BENEATH THE DECK, RIPPING THROUGH THE WOOD AS THOUGH IT WERE MERE PAPER.
KARGA FLEW FROM THE SPLINTERED DECK, SCREAMING AND SWATHED IN FLAMES. HE DISAPPEARED INTO THE SEA.
FIRE MET WATER IN AN EXPLOSION OF BURNING DEBRIS AND STEAM, AND THEN THE WAVE CAME CRASHING DOWN.
FARDEN, WHAT HAVE YOU DONE?
IT WAS KARGA!
GET OFF THE SHIP, LAD! SHE'S DONE FER!
CAP'N GOES DOWN WITH 'IS SHIP IS WHAT I 'ERD! AINT NO WAY I'LL TRY M' CHANCES IN THE SEA TONIGHT!
GODS DAMN IT!
FARDEN SPIED A LARGE WOODEN BOX TIED TO THE RAILING. HE HACKED AT IT WITH HIS SWORD UNTIL IT CAME LOOSE AND THEN STOOD HOLDING IT, WAITING FOR THE SEA TO SWALLOW THE SHIP.
AS THE WATER LURCHED CLOSER, FARDEN NARROWED HIS EYES, STEELED HIS RESERVE, AND THREW THE BOX INTO THE SEA.
THE BRAVE MAGE STEADIED HIMSELF ON THE RAILING AGAINST THE FORCE OF THE STORM AND WAITED FOR HIS MOMENT TO LEAP.
THE TEARBOOK WASN'T ON HIS BED BUT HE FOUND IT HIDING UNDER THE MATRESS IN THE WATER. HE TORE AWAY HIS CLOAK AND BREASTPLATE AND KICKED OFF HIS HEAVY BOOTS SO THAT THEY DIDN'T DROWN HIM.
BUT BEFORE HE COULD MOVE, THERE WAS A DEEP RENDING CRACK FROM SOMEWHERE BEHIND HIM AND SOMETHING HEAVY STRUCK HIM ON THE BACK OF THE HEAD. FARDEN FELL DOWN INTO THE ANGRY SEA AND INTO A DARK DREAM.

WATER FLOODED HIS NOSE AND RAN DOWN HIS THROAT LIKE A RUNAWAY AVALANCHE OF SALTY BLACK LIQUID.
THE SEA PULLED AT HIS HANDS AND FEET AND CLOTHES WITH ICE-COLD FINGERS. HIS WORLD SWITCHED BETWEEN THE ROAR OF THE STORM AND THE INKY DEAFNESS OF UNDERWATER. UP WAS DOWN, AND WATER REPLACED AIR.
BREATHE.
HOLD FAST.
HE FELT SOMETHING UNDER HIS SWOLLEN FINGERS AND GRABBED IT WITH THE LAST VESTIGES OF STRENGTH IN HIS WEARY BODY. ROPES DRAGGED AT RAW CUTS AND LASHED HIM TO THE CRATE THAT KEPT HIM AFLOAT. HIS FOREHEAD FOUND A RESTING PLACE AGAINST THE SALTY WOOD.
DARKNESS.
I AM BREATHING.
BREATHE
FARDEN SHIVERED IN HIS DESERT, AND RUBBED AT HIS COLD ARMS AND LEGS. HIS VAMBRACES LAY RUSTY AND COVERED IN DRYING SEAWEED AT HIS DUSTY FEET. 'BREATHE' SAID A VOICE AND FARDEN TURNED HIS HEAD TO SEE A SKINNY BLACK CAT, SOAKED TO THE BONE,
NOT FOR LONG. . .

' A DRAGON'S CLAWS ARE CURVED AND DEADLY, MUCH LIKE THE STRANGE DAGGERS FROM THE EAST. BEWARE THE TEETH TOO,
'A LARGE DRAGON CAN HAVE UP TO THREE ROWS OF TEETH AND GNASH THEM IN A FEARSOME MANNER BEFORE EATING . '

' A DRAGON MAY HAVE A LONG OR A SHORT TAIL,
BUT EITHER INVARIABLY HAVE A FORKED OR BARBED TIP,
THAT SWISHES AROUND ANGRILY SHOULD A TRAVELLER
CHOOSE TO APPROACH. '

' THEIR SCALES HAVE THE POWER TO MYSTIFY, WITH RIPPLING
COLOURS THAT CAN HYPNOTISE THE UNWARY, AND SOME MAY
EVEN CHANGE COLOUR TO MATCH THEIR BACKGROUNDS. '

' DRAGONS AND THEIR FEATURES: LESSONS IN IDENTIFYING THE SIREN BEAST 'BY MASTER WIRD

A MAN WAS WALKING ALONE ON A ROCKY BEACH.

FROM UNDER A WHITE HOOD PURPLE EYES SCANNED THE GREY WAVES ROLLING UP THE BEACH AND A SCALY NOSE SNIFFED THE SALT AIR. THE MAN WATCHED THE FIRST FEW SHAFTS OF NEW SUNLIGHT PIERCE THE RAIN CLOUDS AND FELT THE FRESH WIND COMING FROM THE WEST ON HIS SKIN.

HE COUGHED A RATTLING HISS, AND WALKED ON, STILL SCANNING THE BEACH. ABRUPTLY, HE STOPPED AND CROUCHED BY A ROCKY OUTCROP. SOMETHING HAD CAUGHT HIS KEEN EYE. A SHAPE LAY IN THE SURF.

WITHIN MOMENTS HE REACHED IT. IT LOOKED LIKE A CRATE, OR A DOOR, A MASS OF ROPES AND RIGGING LYING USELESS AND TANGLED IN THE SAND.

USING HIS SHARP SPEARPOINT, HE PEELED AWAY THE MATTED WEED AND KNOTTED ROPES TO REVEAL THE LONG DEAD EYES OF A GOAT, BLOATED AND SWOLLEN FROM SEAWATER.

THE MAN HOPPED NIMBLY OVER THE STONES. SAND FLEW FROM HIS BOOTS AS HE RAN OVER THE BEACH TOWARDS THE SHAPE.

THE SIREN SPIED SOMETHING THAT LOOKED LIKE A SHOE POKING OUT FROM UNDER A SLIMY SECTION OF WOOD, AND CROUCHED TO INVESTIGATE FURTHER. IT WAS A BOOT, WITH A FOOT AND LEG ATTACHED TO IT.

THE MAN TORE APART THE WOODEN CRATE IN A SPRAY OF GREEN WEED AND WATER TO FIND A BEDRAGGLED CORPSE LYING CURLED UP AND HALF-BURIED IN THE SAND.
HE LOOKED TO BE IN HIS THIRTIES, PROBABLY FROM THE SOUTHEAST, WITH MATTED DARK HAIR AND RED-GOLD VAMBRACES ON HIS ARMS. THE MAN PUT HIS COLD SPEARBLADE TO HIS LIPS IN THOUGHT. THAT'S WHEN HE SAW THE CORPSE'S CHEST MOVING EVER SO SLIGHTLY.
THE MAN PUT A HAND TO THE SODDEN MAN'S CHEST. SOMETHING STIRRED THERE, MAYBE A FAINT HINT OF LIFE AFTER ALL. A SKIPPING HEARTBEAT. RAGGED BREATH.
HE OPENED HIS RED-RIMMED EYES TO FIND A SHINY SPEAR BLADE WAVING IN HIS FACE, AND CLOSED THEM AGAIN TO FIND NOTHING BUT DARKNESS.
THE SIREN BROUGHT A FIST DOWN ON THE MAN'S CHEST, AT THE POINT WHERE THE RIBS JOINED, AND THE WASHED-UP MAN SUDDENLY SPLUTTERED AND COUGHED, RETCHING BILE AND SEAWATER.

WHERE'D YOU FIND HIM?
ON THE BEACH, NEAR THE SOUTH EAST CORNER.
SHOULD HAVE BEEN DEAD, THE POOR BASTARD, BUT SOMEHOW THERE'S STILL LIFE IN HIM.
ARKA, BY THE LOOK OF HIM.
WHAT'S THAT?
I THINK IT'S A CAT, IT WAS NEAR TO WHERE I FOUND HIM.
WELL, WHAT'S IT DOING HERE?
SCALUSSEN VAMBRACES!
I KNOW, THIS ISN'T JUST SOME WASHED UP SAILOR.
THE OTHERS MAY NEED TO HEAR ABOUT THIS.
THE THING'S STILL BREATHING, DON'T ASK ME HOW, IT MUST BELONG TO HIM ...AFTER ALL THE LITTLE THING'S BEEN THROUGH.
YES, YES, AFTER I GET HIM BACK TO HEALTH,
FINE, I'LL HAVE HIM TAKEN TO MY ROOMS AND I'LL SEE WHO HE IS
...IF HE LIVES THAT IS.
I'LL SEND A MESSAGE TO THE OLD DRAGON
FINE WITH ME, GOOD DAY SIR
I WILL DO THAT. . . ONCE HE'S READY TO BE INTERROGATED.
...AND TO YOU

THAT NIGHT THE HEALER QUIETLY PADDED DOWN THE CORRIDOR TO FARDEN'S ROOM, HOLDING NOTHING BUT A TALLOW CANDLE IN HIS HAND.
...A HAND THAT QUIVERED WITH ANTICIPATION...
FOR HE HAD SPIED WHAT LAY UNDER FARDEN'S TUNIC...
CLICK
FARDEN LAY PRONE AND UNCONSCIOUS ON A WOODEN TABLE. SLOWLY THE GREY SIREN CREPT FORWARD.
HE BEGAN TO SLICE THE MAGE'S RAGGED TUNIC.
RRIIPP
THE OLD HEALER GRINNED TO HIMSELF AND SQUINTED. SHAKING HANDS MOVED THE CANDLE CLOSER.
HOURS PASSED AND ITS YELLOW LIGHT BEGAN TO FADE.
CLOTH PARTED AND BETRAYED THE BLACK LETTERING HIDING UNDERNEATH.

AFTER WHAT SEEMED LIKE HOURS, THE HEALER'S EYELIDS FELT LIKE THEY WERE BURNING.
THE CANDLE FELL ...
THE SIREN CURSED AND BENT OVER TO PICK IT UP.
HE FROZE, FEELING SOMETHING BEHIND HIM
THE HEALER SKIDDED AND FELL INTO HIS ROOM, GROPING FOR HIS BED, HIS ONLY REFUGE. GHOSTS THREW FINGERS OF DEAD MEN AT HIS DOOR, CALLING HIS NAME. DARK LETTERS FLEW AROUND HIS HEAD LIKE VENGEFUL CROWS, THEY FLUTTERED THEIR TERRIBLE WINGS, REMINDING HIM OF EVERY BAD THING HE HAD EVER DONE.
A TERRIFIED WAIL BROKE FROM HIS THROAT AS HE BOLTED DOWN THE DARK CORRIDOR.
IN A DARK ROOM DOWN THE CORRIDOR, A MAN SLEPT ON, BREATHING HEAVILY, OBLIVIOUS.
WHY AM I HERE?
I DON'T EVEN KNOW THIS PLACE.
IT'S A LITTLE OF YOU, AND A LITTLE OF ME
WELL, WHO ARE YOU THEN?
I'M TRYING TO HELP.
IF YOU WANTED TO HELP, YOU'D GET ME OUT OF HERE, MAKE THIS PAIN GO AWAY. GET ME BACK TO KRAUSLUNG, OR MAYBE JUST FIND THIS BOOK FOR ME SO I CAN SAVE EMANESKA.
WE NEVER DO. WE NEVER ASK FOR THIS, NOR DO WE EVER COMPLAIN, WE JUST DO AS WE'RE TOLD. IT'S WHAT PEOPLE LIKE YOU AND I DO ; WE FIGHT AND WE NEVER ASK FOR ANYTHING IN RETURN.
LEAVE ME ALONE.
I DON'T NEED YOUR HELP.
I NEVER ASKED FOR THIS.
KEEP AN EYE ON THE WEATHER, FARDEN, THERE'S MORE TO THIS THAN FIRST APPEARS. YOU'VE FOUND THE DRAGONS, NOW LISTEN TO THEM.

FARDEN'S BODY ACHED IN A THOUSAND PLACES.
HIS WRISTS WERE SCREAMING AGAINST THE IRON SHACKLES.
STRAW PRICKED HIS BACK AND THE WALL BEHIND HIS HEAD WAS ICE COLD
...AWAKE FROM SLEEP
THE...MAGE!..
...DARK, DARK SLEEP
WHERE'D YOU GO MAGE?
CLUNK
BE QUIET!
DARK DREAMS YOU HAD,
DARK DAEMON DREAMS!
DREAM DREAM DREAM
LOST IN A DESERT
DO NOT MOVE, ARKA.
HE WANT'S TO SPEAK WITH YOU
BEWARE THE DRAGONS,
MAGE! THEY'LL STEAL
YOUR SOUL!
HAH!
I'VE READ
YOUR MIND!
FELT THE LINES
ON YOUR BACK,
FELT THE WRITING
ON MY FINGERS...
CALLING TO ME

FARDEN WAS SILENT DURING THE JOURNEY, OR DRAGGING, ALL THE WHILE HE DRIFTED IN AND OUT OF FEVERISH CONSCIOUSNES.
HE WAS MANHANDLED THROUGH CORRIDORS. . .
ARKA BOY!
DRAGON FODDER!
ACROSS BUSTLING THOROUGHFARES. . .
SMOOCHY, SMOOCHY, SMOOCHY!
ALONG WIDE BRIDGES. . .
AND FINALLY, DUMPED QUITE UNCEREMONIOUSLY ON THE ICY STONE. ALL WAS SILENT.
UP SPIRALING STEPS. . .
ACROSS WHAT FELT LIKE A COLD, SHINY FLOOR. . .

THERE HAD NOT BEEN MANY TIMES IN HIS LIFE WHEN FARDEN HAD FELT SUCH AWE AND SHOCK, AND BEEN SPEECHLESS BECAUSE OF HIS SURROUNDINGS. THIS WAS ONE OF THOSE TIMES. THE HUMBLED MAGE FELT BEYOND TINY AS HE GAZED UPWARDS AT THE MASSIVE DOMED ROOF SEVERAL HUNDRED FEET ABOVE HIM, PUNCTURED BY SKYLIGHTS.
AT LEAST A THOUSAND LEDGES WERE CARVED INTO THE ROCK, ALL OVER THE HALL. HUGE SCONCES CARVED FROM THE STONE THAT RAN UP AND ALONG THE WALLS LIKE COUNTLESS HONEYCOMBED NESTS.
THERE, LAYING ON A HUGE WOODEN BED OF AUTUMN LEAVES, SPOTLIGHTED BY A LONE SHAFT OF SUNLIGHT, WAS THE OLD DRAGON, FARFALLEN.
'WELL MET AND GOOD WISHES, STRANGER. CAN YOU SPEAK?'
EVERNIA'S TITS! THE OLD DRAGON IS ALIVE!
YES, SIRE,
THE LIGHT OF A THOUSAND LAMPS FLICKERED ALL AROUND HIM, AND DRAGONS, SCORES OF DRAGONS, FILLED THE LOWER LEDGES OF THE GIGANTIC HALL. THEY SQUATTED AND PERCHED ON PILES OF SOFT HAY, SURROUNDED BY LITTLE CANDLES AND PITCHERS OF WATER AND ACCOMPANIED BY THEIR RIDERS.
THE SMELL OF REPTILE AND WOODSMOKE WAS A STRANGE MIX, BUT WELCOME AFTER THE STENCH OF HIS CELL.
FROM WHERE DID YOU COME, THIEF?
BE CALM, SVARTA. SPEAK, GUEST, TELL US,
FARFALLEN'S SIREN WAS A TALL, THIN WILLOW OF A WOMAN. HER STERN FACE WAS LIKE A THIN BLADE, SERIOUS AND COMMANDING. GOLDEN SCALES COVERED HER CHEEKBONES AND THEY RAN IN STRIPES UP HER NECK TO MEET HER CHIN. HER YELLOW EYES PIERCED FARDEN'S AND HE FELT HIMSELF BLINKING WEAKLY.

MY NAME IS FARDEN, I AM AN ARKA MAGE SENT HERE TO SPEAK WITH THE SIREN COUNCIL. MY MASTERS WISH YOU ALL KIND GREETINGS AND EXPRESS THEIR DESIRE TO BRING PEACE BETWEEN OUR TWO PEOPLES.
YOU ARE ONE OF THE WRITTEN.
THAT IS TRUE.
THEN YOU ARE A DANGER TO US ALL!
THE MAGICK THIS MAN HOLDS IN HIS SKIN IS TREACHEROUS. THE HEALER WHO BROUGHT THIS MAGE BACK FROM THE DEAD WAS TURNED TO MADNESS AND LOST HIS MIND TO WHATEVER SPELLS . . .
YOU CAST ON HIM.
I HAVE BEEN UNCONSCIOUS FOR DAYS! THE FIRST TIME I SAW THAT MAN WAS IN MY CELL JUST A MOMENT AGO! WHATEVER HE DID HE DID IT TO HIMSELF AND WITHOUT MY HELP. I'M SURE YOU ALL KNOW WHAT I AM, AND WHAT IS ON MY BACK. HIS MADNESS IS HIS OWN FAULT. NOTHING TO DO WITH ME.
IT IS EVERYTHING TO DO WITH YOU! A STRANGE MAN WASHED UP ON OUR SHORES HALF-DEAD, TAKEN IN BY A KIND HEALER, AND SUDDENLY HE IS TURNED INTO A RAVING LUNATIC? WE SHOULD HAVE LEFT YOU FOR THE GULLS.
MY SHIP WAS ATTACKED ON THE WAY HERE, AND I WAS FORCED TO TAKE MY CHANCES IN THE SEA. SURELY A HAWK HAS ARRIVED WITH NEWS OF MY ARRIVAL?
WE'VE HAD NO SUCH MESSAGE, ARKA. FOR ALL WE KNOW, YOU'RE A ROGUE. A LIAR. AND A THIEF. HOW ELSE COULD YOU HAVE COME BY . . .

SHE REACHED BEHIND HER AND PULLED OUT THE HUGE TEARBOOK, DRY AND SAFE. A GASP CAME FROM THE HALL LIKE A SUDDEN WIND, AS IF A FORGETFUL GUARD HAD LEFT A DOOR OPEN. THE DRAGONS FLAPPED AND MOVED AROUND IN THEIR NESTS. SOME RIDERS PERCHED ON THEIR PARTNERS' LONG SERPENTINE NECKS, LEANING FORWARD TO GET A BETTER VIEW OF THE BOOK.
.... THIS!
THIS MAN WAS FOUND WITH THIS IN HIS CLUTCHES! FARFALLEN'S MEMORIES, LONG STOLEN FROM US AND KEPT BY THE ARKA AS A TROPHY OF THE BATTLE AT RAGJARAK . . .
FARDEN WAS SHOCKED AND RELIEVED AT THE SAME TIME. HE WAS SURE THAT THE TEARBOOK HAD BEEN LOST IN THE WAVES WHEN HE JUMPED SHIP.
YES AND IF THE MESSAGE HAD ARRIVED FROM KRAUSLUNG THEN YOU WOULD KNOW I WAS BRINGING IT AS A GESTURE OF GOOD FAITH! AS A PEACE OFFERING FROM MY PEOPLE!
'YOU'RE A THIEF!' ONE SIREN SOMEWHERE IN THE HALL SHOUTED OUT. 'LIAR!' ANOTHER SHOUTED.
ENOUGH!
I WILL TALK TO THE MAGE, BUT NOT NOW AND NOT HERE. LET HIM EXPLAIN HIMSELF TO ME.'
THE OLD DRAGON REARED UP FROM HIS BED AND SAT UP STRAIGHT WITH A LOUD SCRAPING AND FARDEN FOUND HIMSELF GAZING UP AT HIM. HIS THICK, SPIKY TAIL WHIPPED THE AIR, AND HIS WINGS RUSTLED. HE SAT BACK ON HIS HAUNCHES LIKE A CAT, AND FARDEN FOUND HIMSELF GAZING UP AT HIM.

SVARTA LOOKED LIKE SHE WOULD SAY SOMETHING, BUT FARFALLEN SHOT HER A GLANCE.

MY WORD IS FINAL.

SHE NODDED, AND REMAINED SILENT. THE OTHER DRAGONS RUMBLED THEIR ASSENT. SOME LEAPT INTO THE AIR, BEATING THEIR WINGS WITH HUGE GUSTS OF AIR. FARDEN'S DARK HAIR FLAPPED IN THEIR WIND AS THEY SOARED UPWARDS TO THE SKYLIGHTS IN THE MASSIVE ROOF. FARDEN COULD SEE THE SNOW FLURRYING IN THEIR WAKE.

THE WIND FEELS GOOD TODAY. THE SNOW KEEPS US COLD, YOU SEE. I THINK THAT INSIDE WE'RE ALL FIRE AND HEAT, SO THE NORTH ALWAYS KEEPS US COOL AND COMFORTABLE. THE WEATHER IS BETTER HERE TOO

FARDEN, WALK WITH US.

FARFALLEN'S CLAWS POUNDED THE STONE FLOOR, MAKING THE MAGE'S LEGS QUIVER WITH EVERY STEP.

... FOR FLYING, THAT IS.

REALLY? I THOUGHT KRAUSLUNG WAS BAD. BUT THIS IS FAR TOO COLD FOR ME.

I SUPPOSE THAT'S TRUE. I'M GLAD THAT YOU HAVE YOUR EARBOOK BACK. MANY THINGS HAPPEN IN WAR THAT SHOULDN'T... IF YOU KNOW WHAT I MEAN.

THEY CAME TO AN EXPANSIVE BALCONY THAT LOOKED OVER THE CITADEL OF HJUASSFEN. HIGH OVERHEAD HE COULD SEE DRAGONS CIRCLING THE MOUNTAINTOP, COLOURED SHAPES OF ALL HUES DARTING THROUGH THE WINTRY SKY.

FARDEN TOLD THE STORY OF WHAT HAD HAPPENED AT ARFELL, LEAVING OUT NO DETAIL WHATSOEVER AND REMEMBERING TO BE EXACT AND MIND HIS MANNERS. EVEN THOUGH HE KEPT GLANCING AT FARFALLEN'S CLAWS AND TEETH, WHEN THEY WANDERED ON TO THE TOPICS OF FLYING, AND MAGICK, FARDEN FOUND HIMSELF TALKING OPENLY, AS IF THEY WERE OLD FRIENDS. THEY TALKED FOR AN HOUR, MAYBE MORE, AND WHEN THEY HAD FINISHED, FARFALLEN REMEMBERED SOMETHING.

OH AND SOMETHING ELSE SURVIVED THE SHIPWRECK BESIDES YOU. IT'S IN YOUR ROOM...

FARDEN NODDED, SLIGHTLY CONFUSED, SAID HIS THANKS, AND HEADED TOWARDS THE ROOM WHICH HAD BEEN PREPARED FOR HIM.

A BANGING AWOKE HIM. A PERSISTENT, RESOLUTE KNOCKING THAT STUBBORNLY SHOOK HIS RECENTLY ACQUIRED DOOR.
BANG! BANG! BANG
HE NOTICED HIS SWORD AND SCALUSSEN VAMBRACES HAD BEEN RETURNED. HE DECIDED AGAINST TAKING THE BLADE BUT SLID THE PAIR OF VAMBRACES ONTO HIS WRISTS. THE METAL CONTRACTED SLOWLY AROUND HIS SKIN WITH SLITHERING WHISPERS, LIKE A COILED SNAKE WRAPPING TIGHTLY AROUND A TREE. FARDEN SMILED.
SVARTA STOOD BEHIND IT WITH HER ARMS CROSSED.
DO YOU WANT TO COME IN OR SOMETHING?
WE DON'T HAVE TIME FOR YOUR GAMES, MAGE. FOLLOW ME, AND BE QUICK ABOUT IT.
SVARTA TURNED TO THE LAST PAGE OF THE TEARBOOK. A SINGLE TEAR QUIVERED ON THE VERY END OF FARFALLEN'S CHIN AND HUNG FOR A LONG SECOND BEFORE DROPPING QUIETLY ONTO THE BOOK.
SNAP
FARDEN SILENTLY FOLLOWED SVARTA THROUGH THE MOUNTAIN, AND SOON THEY REACHED A TALL SET OF IRON DOORS. SVARTA STOPPED ABRUPTLY AND SWIVELLED ON ONE HEEL TO FACE HIM.
SVARTA BEGAN TO MOVE FASTER AND FASTER, AND AS THE PAGES FLEW BY, LETTERS BEGAN TO APPEAR. BEFORE LONG, THE YELLOW PAPER WAS COVERED WITH LINES OF INTRICATE SCRIPT. FARFALLEN'S EYES TWITCHED AS HE TRIED TO KEEP PACE WITH SVARTA.
AND ON THEY WENT, UNTIL THE ENTIRE TOME HAD BEEN FILLED WITH MEMORY. SVARTA TOOK A DEEP BREATH AND CLICKED HER LONG FINGERS HIGH ABOVE HER HEAD. AN OLD MAN MATERIALISED OUT OF THE SHADOWS AND CAREFULLY CARRIED THE TEARBOOK AWAY, DISAPPEARING DOWN A DARK CORRIDOR.
UNLESS SOMEONE ASKS YOU A QUESTION, YOU ARE TO BE SILENT IN THIS ROOM.
BRING THE BOOK!
I CAN FEEL THE MEMORIES FLOWING THROUGH ME AGAIN. I HAD NOT REALISED HOW MUCH HAD BEEN LOST TO ME; NAMES, PLACES, KINGS AND QUEENS, ALL COMING BACK TO ME NOW...BIT BY BIT.
FEEL PRIVILEGED, MAGE. NEVER BEFORE HAS AN OUTSIDER WATCHED A DRAGON REBOND WITH HIS TEARBOOK.
IT IS DONE. COME, I WILL SHOW YOU TO THE KITCHENS. I ASSUME WRITTEN EAT?
THE OLD DRAGON RAISED HIS HEAD TO THE CAVERNOUS CEILING AND DREW A LONG BREATH IN THROUGH HIS NOSE. FARDEN WATCHED HIM, FASCINATED, AS HE HELD THE BREATH FOR AN IMPOSSIBLE AMOUNT OF TIME, AND THEN FINALLY EXHALED A BLAST OF BOILING FIRE FROM HIS JAWS. HIS SCALES SHIMMERED, AND THE AIR AROUND HIM RIPPLED LIKE THE AIR AROUND A BLACKSMITH'S FORGE.

SVARTA MARCHED HIM TO THE KITCHEN - A LONG ROOM THAT ROARED WITH THE SOUND OF CONVERSATION AND THE CLATTERING OF PLATES. THE TABLES FILLING THE ROOM WERE CRAMMED WITH SOLDIERS AND SERVANTS.
WHAT?!
SVARTA TURNED AND LEFT HIM IN THE DOORWAY. FARDEN SCOWLED AS THE SIRENS BEGAN TO TURN AND STARE AT HIM, BOWLS AND PLATES FORGOTTEN. SOON ENOUGH, THE WHOLE ROOM WAS LOOKING AT HIM. A DEATHLY QUIET FELL OVER THE TABLES.
THAT SEEMED TO DO THE TRICK. THE MAGE SIGHED AND FETCHED HIMSELF A BOWL OF SOUP. HE SAT DOWN AT THE BACK OF THE ROOM, AGAINST THE WALL.
GODS DAMN THAT SVARTA, HE THOUGHT TO HIMSELF, LEAVING HIM ALONE AMONGST SOLDIERS THAT HATED HIM. IT WAS A SURE WAY TO GET HIM INTO A FIGHT. HE FELT A SHADOW FALL ACROSS HIM AND LOOKED UP TO FIND A GIANT OF A SIREN STANDING OVER HIM.
YOU'RE THE ONE THEY FOUND ON THE BEACH. THE MAGE?
I GUESS SO,
LEAD THE WAY,
FOLLOW ME,
FARDEN BLITHELY WONDERED WHY HIS DECISIONS ALWAYS SEEMED TO BE MADE FOR HIM, LIKE RIDING A WILD BEAST OVER WHICH HE HELD NO POWER NOR SWAY.
I'M FINE HERE, THANK YOU. I DON'T WANT ANY TROUBLE.
YOU'VE COME TO THE WRONG PLACE IF YOU WANT TO BE LEFT ALONE, ARKA. I SUGGEST YOU COME WITH ME IF YOU DON'T WANT TO FIND YOURSELF IN A BRAWL WITH SOME OF THE MORE UNRESTRAINED MEN.
THE WAKE, THE FIRST DRAGON IS OUT FLYING TONIGHT.
THE HUGE MAN LEAD HIM DOWN LONG CORRIDORS AND FLIGHTS OF STAIRS UNTIL THEY CAME TO AN ARCHWAY. THE STRANGER REACHED FOR THE HANDLE OF A WOODEN DOOR SET INTO THE ROCK. THE GUST OF COLD WIND MADE FARDEN'S CLOAK BILLOW WILDLY AROUND HIS LEGS. SNOW DANCED AROUND HIS BOOTS AS HE FOLLOWED THE MAN OUT ONTO A LONG BALCONY.

ANOTHER STORM?
A DISTANT FLASH AMONGST THE LOW CLOUDS CAUGHT FARDEN'S EYE.
THE DARK SHAPE SWOOPED IN A LOW DIVE TO GLIDE OVER THE FOOTHILLS FAR BELOW THEM. FARDEN WATCHED AVIDLY AND WITH BATED BREATH AS THE OBJECT DROPPED FURTHER AND FURTHER UNTIL IT SEEMED TO BE FLYING MERE INCHES ABOVE THE JAGGED BLACK ROCKS OF THE MOUNTAIN.
NO, SOMETHING ELSE ENTIRELY. WAIT,
THERE WAS A MOMENT OF SILENCE. THE WIND HOWLED AND THE SNOW WHIRLED. SUDDENLY A GIGANTIC GOLD SHAPE TORE PAST THE BALCONY AT INCREDIBLE SPEED. THE THUNDERCLAP OF FARFALLEN'S MASSIVE WINGS WAS DEAFENING, AND THE BLAST ALMOST PUSHED THE TWO MEN TO THEIR KNEES.
YOU SEEM HAPPY, MAYBE THAT TEARBOOK HAS DONE YOU SOME GOOD.
THE DRAGON CLIMBED VERTICALLY INTO THE NIGHT SKY AND PIROUETTED ON ONE WING TIP. JUST AS FARDEN THOUGHT THE DRAGON WOULD TUMBLE FROM THE AIR HE SOMERSAULTED AND DOVE FOR THE BALCONY,
IT LOOKED LIKE FARFALLEN WOULD PLUMMET HEADLONG INTO THE ROCKS, BUT AT THE VERY LAST SECOND HIS WINGS BURST OPEN AND THE DRAGON STOPPED IN MIDAIR, GENTLY LETTING HIS WHOLE GARGANTUAN WEIGHT REST ON THE STONE RAILING.
MAYBE IT HAS, MAGE, AND I HAVE YOU TO THANK FOR BRINGING IT BACK TO ME.
HAVE YOU FOUND ANYTHING IN THE TEARBOOK YET?
COME, SVARTA TOLD ME YOU WANTED TO TRAIN. MAYBE IT'LL HELP YOU BLOW OFF SOME STEAM.
MY MEMORIES ARE LONG, FARDEN. ONCE THE TEARBOOK IS READY, IT MAY TAKE MANY DAYS FOR OUR SCHOLARS TO FIND THE LOCATION OF AN ELVEN WELL, IF ONE EVEN EXISTS AT ALL.
EYRUM WILL TAKE YOU TO A ROOM WHERE YOU MAY PRACTISE YOUR MAGICK. I WILL MEET YOU THERE SHORTLY.

ONE MORE TIME, AND KEEP IT THE SAME LEVEL.

FARFALLEN TOOK A DEEP BREATH ONCE MORE AND CROUCHED LOW TO THE FLOOR. THE GREAT DRAGON CLOSED ONE GOLDEN EYE.

IMPRESSIVE, MAGE. NOW, HOW ABOUT YOU CAST ONE OF YOUR FIRE SPELLS AT ME. SEE WHAT HAPPENS.

A STREAM OF FIRE EXPLODED FROM HIS JAWS. WITH LIGHTNING SPEED FARDEN THREW HIS OPEN HANDS OUT TO MEET THE BLAST AND AN INVISIBLE WALL SLAMMED INTO THE FIERY ONSLAUGHT, MERE INCHES IN FRONT OF HIS FINGERS. FEROCIOUS FLAMES SWIRLED AROUND HIM AND LICKED AT HIS BOOTS, BUT HIS INVISIBLE BUBBLE HELD STRONG AGAINST THEM. FARFALLEN CUT SHORT HIS FIRE, AND SMILED.

ARE YOU SURE?

EYRUM SEEMED SURE. THE MAGE SHRUGGED AND STEPPED BACK AGAINST THE NEAREST WALL. HE SLAMMED HIS WRISTS TOGETHER WITH A CLANG. CURLED FINGERS FORMED LIKE A CAGE AROUND NOTHING BUT AIR. A SPARK IGNITED AND SUDDENLY A SWIRLING SPHERE OF FIRE SPUN BETWEEN HIS PALMS. THE FIREBALL RAGED LIKE A TRAPPED SUN. THE AIR TINGLED WITH HEAT AS THE FIRE BURNED BETWEEN HIS GLOWING HANDS.

WHEN THE MAGE WAS READY, HE SPUN ON ONE FOOT AND HURLED THE FIREBALL AT EYRUM, WHO STOOD DEAD STILL ABOUT FORTY PACES FROM HIM. JUST AS THE FIREBALL WAS ABOUT TO BLAST THE SIREN INTO CHARCOAL, EYRUM SIMPLY SHIFTED, WITHOUT ANY OBVIOUS MOVEMENT AT ALL, HE SIMPLY BECAME A BLUR OF A MAN, SLIDING SIDEWAYS ACROSS THE STONE FLOOR AND DODGING THE FLAMES. THE FIREBALL EXPLODED AGAINST THE OPPOSITE WALL WITH A ROAR, CRACKING THE STONE AND MAKING IT GLOW UNDER THE FLAMES.

THE NEXT MORNING, FARDEN AWOKE FEELING FRESHER THAN HE HAD IN DAYS, DESPITE GOING TO BED AS DAWN WAS REACHING OVER THE MOUNTAINOUS HORIZON.

FARDEN SPENT HIS AFTERNOON AIMLESSLY AMBLING THROUGH THE LONG IDENTICAL CORRIDORS CARVED INTO THE ROCK OF THE HUGE MOUNTAIN. FROM SOME OF THE WINDOWS HE FOUND HE COULD PEER DOWN INTO THE CRATERS AND CRAGS OF THE CITY AND WATCH THE HUSTLE AND BUSTLE BELOW.

THEY HAD TALKED FOR HOURS IN THE CANDLELIGHT OF FARFALLEN'S CAVERNOUS HALL, SIPPING WARM WINE AND DARK SPIRITS UNDER THE MARBLE GAZE OF A MIGHTY STATUE; THE SIREN WEATHER- GOD, THRON. FARFALLEN HAD REGALED THEM WITH STORIES OF OLD WARS. EYRUM, TALES OF HIS OLD DRAGON, WHO HAD DIED LONG AGO. THEY DRANK TO HER MEMORY MORE THAN A FEW TIMES.

THE PALACE SEEMED ABUZZ WITH ACTIVITY. FARDEN HAD NO IDEA WHAT WAS GOING ON. HE JUST CARRIED ON WALKING.

THE MAGE SOON FOUND HIMSELF IN THE GREAT HALL TO WHICH HE HAD BEEN DRAGGED ONLY A FEW DAYS AGO. THE SOUND OF SIRENS WORKING AND TALKING WAS A ROAR. A FEW DRAGONS PERCHED IN THEIR NESTS HIGH UP ON THE WALLS, THEIR GREENS, BLUES, AND REDS SPARKLING IN THE DAYLIGHT THAT STREAMED THROUGH THE HOLES IN THE ROOF.
FARDEN WATCHED A WHITE AND GOLD DRAGON FLAP INTO THE HALL. IT DESCENDED SLOWLY, SPIRALLING DOWN WITH SOFT BEATS OF ITS TRANSLUCENT WINGS. IT LANDED RIGHT NEXT TO THE MAGE.
FARDEN WATCHED THE DRAGON FOLD ITS WINGS AND BOW ITS HEAD. IT THEN CLOSED ITS EYES AND SPOKE WITH A LOW AND GENTLE VOICE.
FARFALLEN HAS SEEN TO THAT, MY GOOD MAGE, SOME OF OUR DRAGONS HAVE SPENT YEARS HONING THEIR SKILLS AT READING THE HEARTS AND MINDS OF MEN. THOSE ONES ABOVE US, YOU SEE? THEY WATCH OVER THESE MEN AND THE SOLDIERS, MAKING SURE THAT THEY ARE ALL AS LOYAL AS THEY SHOULD BE.
WELL MET AND GOOD WISHES, FARDEN, I AM BRIGHTSHOW, PARTNER OF LAKKIN. THE OLD DRAGON, IN ALL HIS WISDOM, HAS SUMMONED EVERY SCRIBE AND SCHOLAR IN THE CITY TO COME AND SEARCH THROUGH EVERY HISTORICAL ACCOUNT WE CAN FIND.
GOOD TO MEET YOU BRIGHTSHOW, I TAKE IT FARFALLEN ISN'T WORRIED ABOUT KEEPING THIS MATTER A SECRET THEN? WHAT IF THERE ARE SPIES AMONGST THESE PEOPLE?
YOU DRAGONS NEVER CEASE TO AMAZE ME.
DECORATING THE SMOOTH GRANITE WALLS BETWEEN THE DRAGON NESTS AND THE MANY ARCHWAYS AND CORRIDORS LEADING FROM THE HALL WERE LITTLE FRESCOES AND WALL PAINTINGS.
BEAUTIFULLY CHISELLED AND PAINTED MURALS DEPICTED GREAT BATTLES, HEROIC-LOOKING DRAGONS, STRANGE ANCIENT BEASTS, SOME OF WHICH FARDEN HAD NEVER SEEN BEFORE, AND GREAT LANDSCAPES OF ICE AND SNOW THAT SEEMED AS REAL AS LOOKING OUT OF A WINDOW.
IN ANOTHER THOUSAND YEARS IT WILL ALL HAVE CHANGED AGAIN, AND ANOTHER LIKE YOU WILL BE STANDING HERE LOOKING AT PICTURES OF ANCIENT MEN AND LOST DRAGONS. THE WORLD MOVES ON. IT IS THE WAY OF THINGS. COME, LET US SEND YOUR MESSAGE TO THE ARKA.
'SAFE AND WELL IN THE NORTH, SIRENS PEACEFUL, SEARCHING FOR THE WELL NOW, RETURNING TODAY OR TOMORROW BY QUICKDOOR WITH NEWS. BEWARE SPIES IN MIDST, SARUNN WAS DESTROYED BY A DARK SORCERER AND ALL HANDS WERE LOST. TRUST NO ONE.'
FARDEN SCRATCHED A BRIEF MESSAGE IN RED INK AND TINY LETTERS. IT STAINED HIS FINGERS AS HE WROTE.

BRIGHTSHOW AND FARDEN WENT BACK TO THE HALL, WHERE FARFALLEN, SVARTA, EYRUM, AND A FEW OTHER DRAGONS HAD GATHERED IN THE CENTRE OF THE HUGE MASS OF TABLES.
WHAT DO YOU MEAN WEEKS?
IF IT WILL TAKE WEEKS, THEN IT WILL TAKE WEEKS. HOWEVER! UNDERSTAND THAT WE ARE ALL IN GREAT DANGER, AND YOUR LIVES DEPEND ON FINDING THIS WELL BEFORE IT IS TOO LATE. DO YOU HEAR ME?
WHAT?
EVEN THE OLDEST OF OUR TEARBOOKS DON'T GO BACK AS FAR AS THE OLD DRAGONS. YOUR HIGHNESS, NONE OF THE SCROLLS OR PARCHMENTS HERE HAVE HINTED AT A WELL, THEREFORE IT MUST BE...
NOW, FARDEN, YOU GO HOME. WE WILL CONTINUE TO SEARCH THROUGH MY MEMORIES AND FIND THIS ELF WELL.
BUT YOU SAID YOURSELF IT WOULD TAKE WEEKS,
IT MUST BE IN YOUR DRAGON'S MEMORIES, AND THAT'S THE PROBLEM, IT IS TAKING FAR LONGER THAN WE EXPECTED...
MAYBE SO, BUT IF I AND SVARTA AND THE OTHERS HELP THEM SEARCH, THEN YOU SHALL HAVE YOUR ANSWER WITHIN A WEEK
THEN I WILL RETURN TO KRAUSLUNG. THE ARKA WILL NEED TO BE READY JUST IN CASE
KNOCK KNOCK
I HAVE A PARTING GIFT FOR YOU, BEFORE YOU GO.
WHEN A DRAGON DIES, THEIR SCALES SOAK UP AND HOLD ON TO THEIR LUCK.
ARE YOU READY TO GO?
FINE.
I CAN'T TAKE THIS, EYRUM, IT'S FROM YOUR DRAGON...
LOOK AFTER MY CAT, IF YOU CAN.
FARDEN WENT TO HIS LITTLE ROOM TO GATHER UP HIS THINGS. TWO FRESH TUNICS AND A NEW BLACK CLOAK WERE DELIVERED TO HIM.
THANK YOU.
YOU CAN RELAX NOW THAT I'M GOING BACK HOME.
EYRUM HAD TOLD FARDEN OF HOW HE HAD LOST HIS DRAGON IN THE WAR. FARDEN WAS SHOCKED, HONOURED, AND CONFUSED ALL AT THE SAME TIME.
I HAVE A FEELING YOU NEED IT MORE THAN I DO.
UNLIKELY, I HAVE A TEARBOOK TO SCOUR THROUGH,.
DOWN AT THE WEST DOCKS, THE WEATHER WAS FAR FROM GRACIOUS. THE MAGE STOOD BESIDE FARFALLEN. SPURS OF BLACK ROCK FORMED THE GATEWAY OF THE QUICKDOOR. IT THRUMMED WITH THE ENERGY AND SEA-SPRAY FIZZED INTO STEAM ON ITS HAZY SURFACE.
I HOPE TO SEE YOU FLYING OVER THE OSSFEN MOUNTAINS IN A WEEK.
YOU JUST CONCENTRATE ON GETTING THE ARKA READY, WELL DO OUR BIT.
GODS SPEED YOU FARDEN!
FARDEN TOOK A DEEP BREATH AS HE WALKED UP TO THE QUICKDOOR. THE DRAGONS ROARED AS HE STEPPED OVER THE THRESHOLD. EVERYTHING MELTED INTO ONE WHITE BLUR.

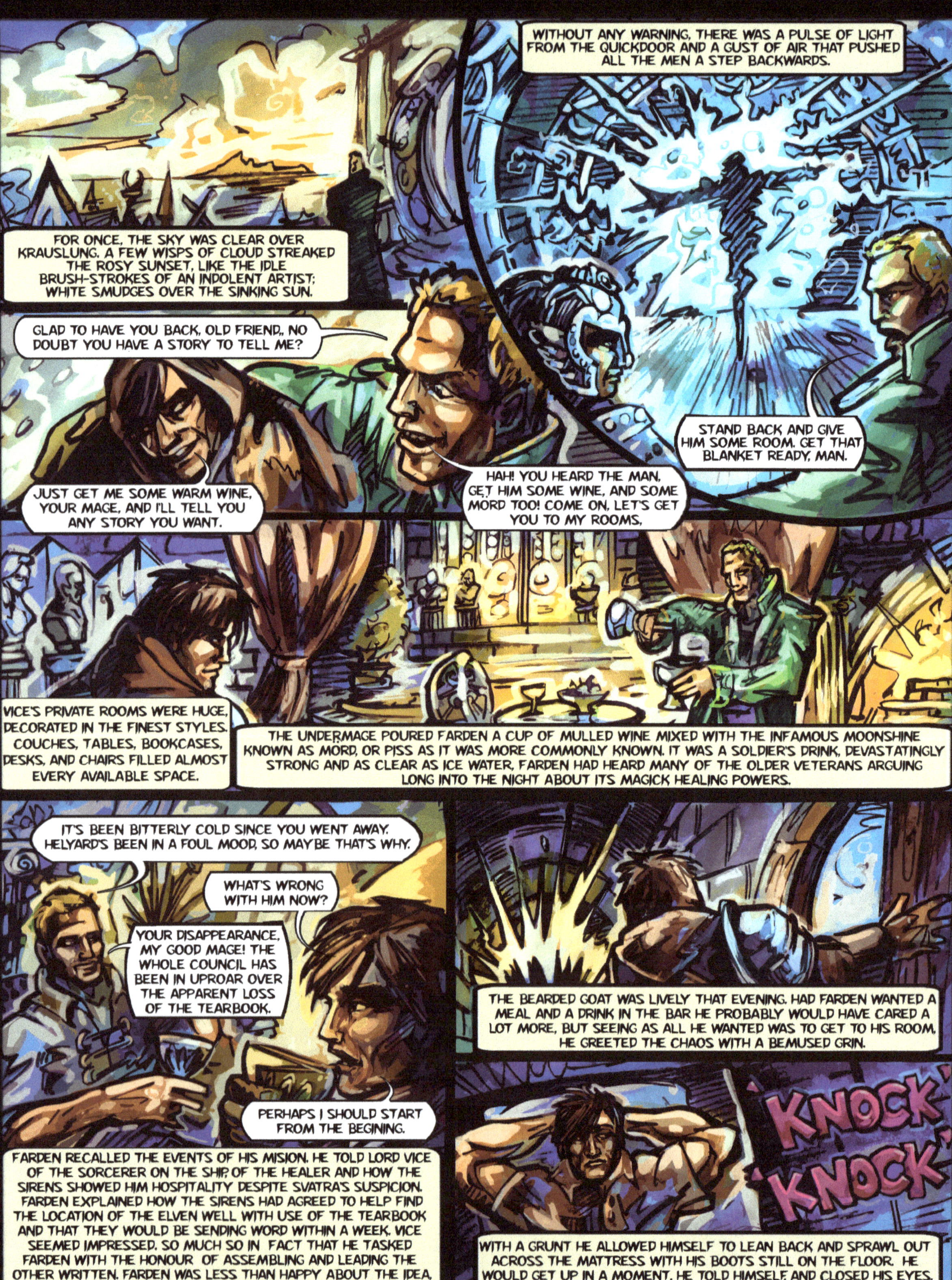

WITHOUT ANY WARNING, THERE WAS A PULSE OF LIGHT FROM THE QUICKDOOR AND A GUST OF AIR THAT PUSHED ALL THE MEN A STEP BACKWARDS.
FOR ONCE, THE SKY WAS CLEAR OVER KRAUSLUNG. A FEW WISPS OF CLOUD STREAKED THE ROSY SUNSET, LIKE THE IDLE BRUSH-STROKES OF AN INDOLENT ARTIST; WHITE SMUDGES OVER THE SINKING SUN.
GLAD TO HAVE YOU BACK, OLD FRIEND, NO DOUBT YOU HAVE A STORY TO TELL ME?
STAND BACK AND GIVE HIM SOME ROOM. GET THAT BLANKET READY, MAN.
JUST GET ME SOME WARM WINE, YOUR MAGE, AND I'LL TELL YOU ANY STORY YOU WANT.
HAH! YOU HEARD THE MAN, GET HIM SOME WINE, AND SOME MORD TOO! COME ON, LET'S GET YOU TO MY ROOMS.
VICE'S PRIVATE ROOMS WERE HUGE, DECORATED IN THE FINEST STYLES. COUCHES, TABLES, BOOKCASES, DESKS, AND CHAIRS FILLED ALMOST EVERY AVAILABLE SPACE.
THE UNDERMAGE POURED FARDEN A CUP OF MULLED WINE MIXED WITH THE INFAMOUS MOONSHINE KNOWN AS MORD, OR PISS AS IT WAS MORE COMMONLY KNOWN. IT WAS A SOLDIER'S DRINK, DEVASTATINGLY STRONG AND AS CLEAR AS ICE WATER. FARDEN HAD HEARD MANY OF THE OLDER VETERANS ARGUING LONG INTO THE NIGHT ABOUT ITS MAGICK HEALING POWERS.
IT'S BEEN BITTERLY COLD SINCE YOU WENT AWAY. HELYARD'S BEEN IN A FOUL MOOD, SO MAYBE THAT'S WHY.
WHAT'S WRONG WITH HIM NOW?
YOUR DISAPPEARANCE, MY GOOD MAGE! THE WHOLE COUNCIL HAS BEEN IN UPROAR OVER THE APPARENT LOSS OF THE TEARBOOK.
THE BEARDED GOAT WAS LIVELY THAT EVENING. HAD FARDEN WANTED A MEAL AND A DRINK IN THE BAR HE PROBABLY WOULD HAVE CARED A LOT MORE, BUT SEEING AS ALL HE WANTED WAS TO GET TO HIS ROOM, HE GREETED THE CHAOS WITH A BEMUSED GRIN.
PERHAPS I SHOULD START FROM THE BEGINING.
KNOCK KNOCK
FARDEN RECALLED THE EVENTS OF HIS MISION. HE TOLD LORD VICE OF THE SORCERER ON THE SHIP, OF THE HEALER AND HOW THE SIRENS SHOWED HIM HOSPITALITY DESPITE SVATRA'S SUSPICION. FARDEN EXPLAINED HOW THE SIRENS HAD AGREED TO HELP FIND THE LOCATION OF THE ELVEN WELL WITH USE OF THE TEARBOOK AND THAT THEY WOULD BE SENDING WORD WITHIN A WEEK. VICE SEEMED IMPRESSED. SO MUCH SO IN FACT THAT HE TASKED FARDEN WITH THE HONOUR OF ASSEMBLING AND LEADING THE OTHER WRITTEN. FARDEN WAS LESS THAN HAPPY ABOUT THE IDEA, BUT HE COULD NOT REFUSE.
WITH A GRUNT HE ALLOWED HIMSELF TO LEAN BACK AND SPRAWL OUT ACROSS THE MATTRESS WITH HIS BOOTS STILL ON THE FLOOR. HE WOULD GET UP IN A MOMENT, HE TOLD HIMSELF, AND CLOSED HIS EYES. THERE CAME A QUIET KNOCK AT THE DOOR.

IN THE DARK HALLWAY STOOD A VERY COLD AND VERY WET CHESKA, HER HAIR BEDRAGGLED AND DRIPPING, COAT GRIPPED TIGHTLY AROUND HER.
EXPECTING SOMEONE?
CHESKA! COME IN, YOU LOOK LIKE YOU'RE FREEZING.
I'VE BEEN WAITING FOR HOURS, FARDEN, EVER SINCE I HEARD YOU WERE BACK.
MY RITUAL STARTS TOMORROW.
VICE AND I HAD THINGS TO GO OVER, THERE WAS WINE. IT'S GOING TO BE A DIFFICULT DAY FOR US TOMORROW.
I JUST HOPE YOU KNOW WHAT YOU'RE DOING CHESKA.
YOU KNOW I DO.
I HOPE SO.
SEE, YOU DO CARE ABOUT ME. SO HOW WAS NELSKA?
FARDEN PROCEEDED TO GO OVER EVERYTHING HE COULD REMEMBER ABOUT THE SIRENS AND THEIR DRAGONS. HE TOLD HER ABOUT SVARTA, BUT NOT FARFALLEN, AND TRIED TO LOOSELY EXPLAIN WHY IT WAS SO IMPORTANT THAT THEY FIND A DARK ELF WELL. FARDEN TRUSTED HER, BUT SOME THINGS COULD BE LEFT UNTIL THIS WAS ALL OVER. FARDEN LIT THE FIRE.
YOU'RE COLD.
THAT WAS UNNECESSARY.
BUT IT'S WHY I'M SO GOOD; I'M ALWAYS PRACTISING.
I COULD GIVE YOU A RUN FOR YOUR COIN.
WHAT DID YOU CHOOSE ANYWAY?
ILLUSION AND SPARK. WHAT DID YOU CHOOSE?
YOU ALREADY KNOW. FIRE AND LIGHT,
. . ,SPARK AND QUAKE.
WHAT ABOUT THE OTHER TWO?
FARDEN RELUCTANTLY TOLD CHESKA OF THE EXTRA TWO MAGICK RUNES IN HIS TATTOO. FARDEN HAD BEEN ONE OF THE LAST WRITTEN TO RECEIVE FOUR RUNES. ONLY DURNUS AND VICE KNEW THAT SECRET.
I'M SCARED, FARDEN...
AT THAT MOMENT THE PAIR LOST THEMSELVES IN A FLURRY OF PASSION.
CLOTHES FELL TO THE FLOOR. WORDS HAD BECOME USELESS. ONLY THEIR ACTIONS COULD SPEAK.
THE SHADOWS BURNT AWAY FROM THE CORNERS OF FARDEN'S MIND AND HE FORGOT EVERYTHING EXCEPT HER, AND SHE WAS A BRIGHT ISLAND, LIKE A CANDLE IN HIS DARKNESS.
AS THE FIRE DIED, THEY LET THE DARKNESS TAKE THEM, EXISTING AS ONE IN THE SHADOWS. FARDEN LET HIMSELF DRIFT INTO A BOTTOMLESS SLEEP.

THE WIND WAS BITINGLY COLD, TEARING AT THE BLACK CLOAK OF THE FIGURE STANDING IN THE DARKNESS ON THE SHORE LIKE THE TEETH OF A THOUSAND RATS, INVISIBLE AND HUNGRY.
THE HUGE FACE OF THE FORTRESS OF HJAUSSFEN TOWERED ABOVE HIM. THE BLACK GRANITE CLIFFS WERE ALMOST INVISIBLE AGAINST THE DARK SKY, BUT A FEW YELLOW TORCHES GLITTERED FROM A HANDFUL OF WINDOWS, BETRAYING THE CITADEL. FOR THE QUIET MAN STANDING ALONE ON THE BEACH, THE WEATHER WAS PERFECT.
IN THE DARKER SHADOWS OF THE CLIFF FACE A SIREN STOOD GUARD, SPEAR HELD FIRMLY AND LOW BY HIS SIDE.
BY THE TIME HE HIT THE GROUND HE WAS DEAD.
ON PEAK OF THE CLIFFS, AT THE TOP OF A WINDING STAIRCASE, WAS A LITTLE DOOR CUT INTO THE ROCK. A LONE SOLDIER STOOD STAMPING HIS FEET TO TRY TO KEEP WARM.
A NOISE REACHED HIS KEEN EARS OVER THE HOWLING OF THE WIND, THE SOUND OF BOOTS ON STONE.
A YELL CAUGHT IN HIS THROAT AS A BOLT OF LIGHTNING SLAMMED INTO HIS CHEST AND THREW HIM BACKWARDS WITH A CRACK OF THUNDER.
THE DOOR SPLINTERED INTO A THOUSAND PIECES, AND THE AIR WAS DRIVEN FROM HIS LUNGS.

SOON A BELL RANG SOMEWHERE DEEP IN THE MOUNTAIN, AND THE CORRIDORS CAME ALIVE WITH SOLDIERS, SWARMING LIKE ANTS.
BUT THE STAIRS SLOWED THEM AND THE MURDERER WAS FAR AHEAD, HIGH UP AT THE TOP OF THE PALACE.
HE MADE HIS WAY TO THE STATUE OF THE WINGED GOD AT THE END OF THE HALL, AND THE LITTLE STONE TABLE SITTING NEAR IT.
THE TEARBOOK AND A FLOCK OF PAPERS SAT ON IT, BARELY ILLUMINATED BY THE FLICKERING CANDLES AROUND THE SHRINE.
THE HOODED FIGURE SEIZED THE TEARBOOK, AND STUFFED THE PARCHMENT BESIDE IT INTO A SATCHEL, MAKING SURE HE GOT ALL OF IT.
THE SOUND OF BELLS AND HORNS SHOOK THE FORTRESS AROUND HIM. IT WAS TIME TO LEAVE.
HE REACHED INSIDE HIS TUNIC AND BROUGHT FORTH A GOLDEN OBJECT. IT GLITTERED BRIGHTLY IN THE LIGHT FROM THE CANDLES.
THE SIRENS BELLOWED AND GAVE CHASE BUT THE MAN WAS FAST. HE DISAPPEARED DOWN AN ADJOINING CORRIDOR.
THE BRIGHT CORRIDOR WAS FULL OF THE SOUNDS OF ARMOUR AND CLANGING WEAPONS, AND JUST AS HE EMERGED FROM THE DARK HALL A GROUP OF SOLDIERS CAME AROUND A CORNER AND SPOTTED HIM.

OTHER SOLDIERS JOINED THE HUNT, SPURRED BY THE SHOUTS AND CRIES. SOON ENOUGH, THE ENTIRE PALACE RACED AFTER THE HOODED INTRUDER.
THEY FOLLOWED THE TRAIL OF DEAD BODIES LEFT ON STAIRCASES AND IN DOORWAYS, OR SLUMPED AGAINST WALLS.
THE SIRENS WANTED BLOOD NOW, AND THE INTRUDER KNEW IT. HE TURNED A CORNER TO FIND A PHALANX OF ARMOURED SOLDIERS BLOCKING THE CORRIDOR, TEETH BARED AND SCALES FLUSHED..
THE CORRIDOR WAS THE ONLY WAY OUT OF THIS SECTION OF THE PALACE, BUT THE MAN HAD ONE MORE CARD TO PLAY.
MERE SECONDS BEFORE THE SPEARS AND SWORDS CUT HIM INTO PIECES, THE STRANGER SWUNG HIS GOLD DISK IN A WIDE CIRCLE AND COMPLETELY DISAPPEARED, SLIPPING INTO THE BOUNCING, SHAKING AIR AND VANISHING.
BACK ON THE BEACH, THERE CAME A LOUD WHIPCRACK, LIKE A TREE SNAPPING IN HALF. THE AIR SPLIT IN TWO, AND A HOODED MAN WAS SPAT OUT INTO THE DARKNESS.
SHOUTS RANG OUT FROM THE CLIFFS BEHIND HIM, AND HE HEARD THE SOUND OF ARROWS AGAINST THE WIND.
A RANCOUROUS SMIRK CREPT ACROSS HIS LIP, AND HE LOOKED AGAIN AT THE DISK IN HIS HAND.
WITH A CHUCKLE, THE HOODED MAN FLUNG IT ONTO THE BEACH, TOWARDS THE CHARGING SIRENS. IT CLANGED ON THE SLIPPERY STONES.
PERHAPS IT WAS THE CURRENT AND THE WINDS THAT DRAGGED THE INTRUDERS FROM THE SHORE, OR MAYBE IT WAS SOMETHING TO DO WITH THE MAGE AT THE FRONT OF THE BOAT, BUT EITHER WAY THEY SPED ACROSS THE CHOPPY SEAS AND INTO THE STORMY NIGHT.

FARDEN AWOKE WHEN THE BRIGHT SUNLIGHT CLIMBED OVER THE ROOFTOPS AND PIERCED THE DARKNESS OF HIS ROOM. HE ROLLED OVER AND REACHED OUT FOR THE BEAUTIFUL GIRL IN HIS BED BUT FOUND ONLY CHESKA'S FJORTLA. SHE HAD LEFT IT FOR HIM TO KEEP, UNTIL SHE HAD PASSED THROUGH THE RITUAL.
FARDEN SPOTTED A FAMILIAR FACE AMONGST THE CROWD.
FARDEN ASKED A NEARBY GUARD THE REASON FOR ALL THE CHAOS.
WHATEVER'S GOING ON HERE, IT'S ALL GONE TO SHIT, I'LL TELL YOU THAT. THIALF AND THE OTHERS ARE OVER THERE. FREIDD IS COMING SOON.
MODREN, AT LEAST THERE'S ONE SANE PERSON AMONGST THIS MESS.
EVEN THOUGH HE WAS ONLY A SHORT DISTANCE FROM THE ARKATHEDRAL, IT HAD TAKEN HIM ALMOST AN HOUR TO REACH THE FORTRESS. THE STREETS WERE BUSTLING, PANICKED ALMOST, AND THE GRAND MARBLE ATRIUM OF THE ARKATHEDRAL WAS NO DIFFERENT, CRAMMED WITH ALL MANNER OF GUARD, MAGE, AND KRAUSLUNG CITIZEN.
HAVEN'T YOU 'EARD? THE DRAGONS ARE COMIN' TO KRAUSLUNG!
FARDEN!
A BOOMING VOICE SUDDENLY ECHOED ACROSS THE ATRIUM.
THOSE BLOODY SIRENS ARE UP IN ARMS ABOUT SOMETHING, AND THEY WON'T TELL US WHAT UNTIL THEY GET HERE, WHICH IS ANY MINUTE NOW. THEY'VE THREATENED WAR, FARDEN. THE ARKMAGES ARE FURIOUS, AS AM I, FARDEN, WITH YOU.
WHY DIDN'T YOU TELL ME ABOUT THE OLD DRAGON? IMAGINE MY SURPRISE WHEN I WAS TOLD BY THE ARKMAGES THAT THE OLD FIEND IS STILL ALIVE. HELYARD ACCUSED ME OF BEING IN LEAGUE WITH THEM!
FARDEN AND MODREN FOLLOWED IN VICE'S FURIOUS WAKE, ELBOWING THEIR WAY THROUGH CROWDS, UP STAIRWELLS, AND THROUGH CORRIDORS. AT LONG LAST THEY REACHED THE GREAT COUNCIL HALL.
HE KNOWS THAT'S NOT TRUE; I CAN EXPLAIN IT ALL.
BETTER YOU THAN ME, MATE
ALL AROUND THEM, COUNCIL MEMBERS ARGUED AND BELLOWED AT THE TOP OF THEIR VOICES, THROWING THEIR OPINIONS BACK AND FORTH WHILE THE ARKMAGES SAT IN THEIR TALL WHITE THRONES AND TALKED AGITATEDLY BETWEEN THEMSELVES.

SILENCE!
I HOPE TO THE GODS YOU BEAR SOME SORT OF EXPLANATION FOR THIS CHAOS, FARDEN.
YOUR MAGES, I HAVE NO IDEA WHY THE SIRENS ARE ON THEIR WAY TO KRAUSLUNG, OR WHY THEY ARE THREATENING WAR
SO WE HEARD FROM LORD VICE THIS MORNING, WHEN HE GAVE US YOUR REPORT...
WHICH WE MIGHT ADD, LEFT OUT THE IMPORTANT FACT THAT FARFALLEN IS STILL ALIVE. I'M ASSUMING THAT NEITHER YOU NOR THE UNDERMAGE CAN EXPLAIN THIS?
WHEN I LEFT NELSKA, THEY ASSURED ME THAT OUR TWO PEOPLE WERE AT PEACE.
IT WAS THEN THAT DISTANT HORNS RANG OUT ALONG THE WALLS OF KRAUSLUNG. THE MAGICK COUNCIL MURMURED NERVOUSLY.
THE DRAGONS HAD ARRIVED.
ONE BY ONE, FARFALLEN AND HIS GLITTERING ENTOURAGE, DROPPED THROUGH THE GREAT HALL'S ENORMOUS SKYLIGHT.
WELL MET AND GOOD WISHES, YOUR MAGES. IT HAS BEEN A LONG TIME SINCE WE LAST MET, AND I REGRET THAT IT IS UNDER SUCH DARK CIRCUMSTANCES THAT WE GREET EACH OTHER AGAIN.
IT SEEMS TO BE THE DESTINY OF OUR PEOPLES, TO ALWAYS BE AT WAR, OLD DRAGON.

YOUR MESSAGE DID NOT MENTION THE PURPOSE OF YOUR VISIT.
BETRAY YOU...?
WE ARE HERE FOR AN EXPLANATION, ARKMAGES, AS TO WHY YOU HAVE ATTEMPTED TO BETRAY US.
DON'T PLAY GAMES, ARKMAGE. WE KNOW THAT YOU WERE BEHIND THE THEFT OF FARFALLEN'S TEARBOOK. WE KNOW IT WAS YOU WHO SENT THE MURDERER INTO OUR MIDST, WHO KILLED A SCORE OF MY SIRENS. WE DEMAND RETRIBUTION!
YOUR ACCUSATION MAKES NO SENSE. WHY WOULD WE SEND YOU THE TEARBOOK ONLY TO STEAL IT BACK AGAIN? AND WHY ARE THE ARKA BEING SO READILY HELD TO BLAME FOR THESE CRIMES?
YOU SHOULD KNOW, ADDREN, IT WAS ONE OF THE ARKMAGES THAT COMMITTED THIS CRIME.
THIS IS AN OUTRAGE! HOW DARE YOU ACCUSE THE ARKMAGES OF SUCH A LIE! WHAT PROOF DO YOU HAVE, IF ANY, OF THIS RIDICULOUS ACCUSATION?
YOU WANT PROOF, VICE? ARKMAGES?
THIS IS RIDICULOUS.
HERE IS YOUR PROOF!
YOUR MAGES?
EXCUSE ME?
HELYARD? I THINK AN EXPLANATION IS NEEDED...
IT WAS A WEIGHT, AN ENCHANTED SYMBOL OF OFFICE CARRIED BY ALL ARKMAGES SINCE ANYONE COULD BEAR TO REMEMBER THERE WERE TWO OF THEM; ONE FOR ADDREN AND ONE FOR HELYARD.
SLOWLY AND CAREFULLY, ADDREN PULLED FORTH A GOLD DISK FROM UNDER HIS ROBE, A DISK THAT WAS IDENTICAL TO THE ONE LYING ON THE FLOOR.

ALL EYES TURNED ON HELYARD.
THIS IS RIDICULOUS! GODS DAMN IT, CAN'T YOU HEAR HOW ABSURD THIS ACCUSATION IS, ÁDDREN? I WAS HERE IN KRAUSLUNG FOR THE ENTIRE EVENING, ASK ANYONE! THIS IS NONSENSE! I AM INNOCENT OF THIS CRIME!
LIES! IT WAS STOLEN AND...
THEN EXPLAIN THIS!
WITH A SNARL, SVARTA KICKED THE WEIGHT AGAINST THE FOOT OF THE MARBLE THRONES.
VICE WALKED CALMLY FORWARD TO STAND BESIDE ÁDDREN, AND TO WHISPER IN HIS EAR. FARDEN WONDERED HOW MUCH PRIVACY THEY COULD MUSTER UNDER THE WATCHFUL EYES OF THE DRAGONS AND THE REST OF THE HALL. EARS WERE PRICKED.
STOLEN! FROM ONE OF THE ARKMAGES? EVEN IF IT HAD BEEN TAKEN FROM YOU, WHO ELSE CAN USE IT, HELYARD? WHO?
ÁDDREN'S VOICE SOUNDED LIKE A TWIG SNAPPING IN A SILENT FOREST
THIS IS AN OUTRAGE!
THIS ISN'T OVER, SIREN! I'M WARNING YOU! ÁDDREN!
GUARDS, REMOVE THE ARKMAGE FROM THE HALL
HELYARD'S VOICE ECHOED AROUND THE HALL LONG AFTER THE GREAT GOLDEN DOORS SHUT WITH A BANG. THE COUNCIL STOOD IN SHOCKED SILENCE.

YOU'VE GOT WHAT YOU CAME FOR, HELYARD HAS BEEN EXPOSED AND WILL BE PUNISHED ACCORDINGLY.
NOT SO FAST, UNDERMAGE, WE CAME HERE FOR ANSWERS.
AND WHAT ANSWERS WOULD THEY BE!? YOU'VE BROUGHT THIS MAGICK COUNCIL TO ITS KNEES AND HAD ONE OF THE ARKMAGES IMPRISONED FOR TREASON, WHAT MORE COULD YOU POSSIBLY WANT!
I THINK WE HAVE ARGUED ENOUGH FOR ONE DAY, BUT THE QUESTION STILL REMAINS WHETHER HELYARD WAS WORKING ALONE, OR IF WE SHOULD STILL READY OURSELVES FOR THE SUMMONING OF THIS CREATURE?
ALBION, HELYARD HAS BEEN TRAVELLING THERE AT NIGHT FOR THE PAST FEW WEEKS. I THOUGHT NOTHING OF IT UNTIL NOW.
BECAUSE YOU HAVE BEEN SO LOYAL TO THE ARKA IN THE FACE OF SUCH BETRAYAL, I NOW WANT YOU TO HOLD ONTO THIS, SO THAT I MAY BE EXEMPT FROM ANY BLAME.
MY SUPERIOR AT THE ARKABBEY, THE VAMPYRE DURNUS IS ONE OF THE FINEST HISTORIANS AND SCHOLARS THE ARKA HAVE. AND I THINK HE WOULD BE INVALUABLE IN HELPING TO FIND THE ELVEN WELL. IF I MIGHT ASK A FAVOUR OF THE SIRENS, YOUR MAGE, I WOULD LIKE IT IF BRIGHTSHOW FLEW ME TO THE ARKABBEY IN ALBION.
HE WENT TO ALBION THE NIGHT BEFORE I LEFT FOR NELSKA THE SORCERER ON THE SHIP ALSO HAD AN ALBION ACCENT.
HE WENT TO KILTYRIN TWO NIGHTS AGO, AND FIDLARIG BEFORE THAT. THIS HAS TO BE WHAT WE'RE LOOKING FOR.
VICE, YOU WILL TAKE THE ARMY TO THE PORT OF DUNYRA BY SHIP OR BY QUICKDOOR, FIND THAT WELL AND DESTROY IT. I WILL NOT ALLOW THESE TRAITORS TO SUMMON THIS CREATURE, IT MUST BE KILLED AT ALL COSTS! THE WRITTEN CAN QUICKDOOR TO THE PORT OF DUNYRA, THE COUNCIL IS NOW DISMISSED, THE DRAGONS AND THEIR RIDERS MAY STAY, AS CAN YOU FARDEN.
WE CAN HAVE DRAGONS SEARCHING FOR THE WELL IN A FEW HOURS.
IT MAKES SENSE, AND I SEE NO PROBLEM WITH IT. BE QUICK THOUGH, FARDEN, WE HAVE NO TIME TO WASTE.
FARDEN BOWED ONCE MORE AND THANKED THE ARKMAGE. HE TOOK THE WEIGHT, MARVELLING AT ITS LIGHTNESS, AND SLIPPED IT INSIDE HIS CLOAK.
FARDEN LEFT THE ARKATHEDRAL TO RETURN TO THE BEARDED GOAT AND GATHER SUPPLIES. AFTER, HE STOPPED TO HAVE HIS SWORD SHARPENED IN THE MARKET. THERE, HE SPIED A TINY STALL HIDING UNDER THE PORCH OF AN OLD BUILDING. ITS VENDOR, A THIN, WIRY WOMAN, SHOWED HIM HER WARES: PRECIOUS STONES AND GEMS FROM THE WILDS. SHE POINTED HIM TO A DAEMONSTONE, SO SHE CALLED IT. A GOLD STONE AND A BEAUTIFUL GIFT FOR A WIFE OR MISTRESS. FARDEN BOUGHT IT FOR CHESKA, FOR LUCK.
I'LL MEET YOU IN FRONT OF THE MAIN GATES OUTSIDE YOUR CITY, FARDEN, AS SOON AS NIGHT FALLS.
FARDEN SMILED AT THE DRAGON AND BOWED.
ALMOST AN HOUR LATER HE REACHED THE ARKATHEDRAL GATES. MODREN WAS WAITING FOR HIM IN THE RAIN.
ARE THE WRITTEN GOING TO BE READY IN TIME? AS MUCH AS I DISTRUST THAT GOLDEN LIZARD, FARFALLEN IS RIGHT: WHOEVER HELYARD WAS WORKING WITH COULD POTENTIALLY RELEASE THE CREATURE AT ANY TIME.
I'LL ASSEMBLE THEM NOW AND GET THEM THROUGH THE QUICKDOOR TO DUNYRA AS SOON AS POSSIBLE. WE'LL BE AT FIDLARIG BY NIGHTFALL.
YOU WAIT UNTIL WE GET INSIDE, MATE, I HAVEN'T SEEN SOMETHING LIKE THIS IN A LONG TIME.

MODREN HAD BEEN RIGHT. THE MAIN ATRIUM OF THE ARKATHEDRAL WAS CRAMMED WITH WRITTEN. FARDEN WASN'T SURE HE'D SEEN SO MANY OF THEM IN HIS LIFETIME, AND HIS HEART FILLED WITH PRIDE. THEY WERE ARMED, EQUIPPED, EAGER, AND READY TO FIGHT, EYES BLAZING WITH THE ANTICIPATION OF BATTLE. FARDEN LOOKED OVER THE MULTITUDE OF DIFFERENT FACES, PICKING OUT A FEW HE HAD FOUGHT WITH MANY TIMES, OTHERS HE HAD NEVER SEEN BEFORE.

THE ONLY CHANCE WE HAVE IS TO FIND A DARK ELF WELL BEFORE THEY DO, AND THAT'S WHY WE'RE GOING TO ALBION TONIGHT, TO THE PORT OF DUNYRA. WE ALL KNOW THAT WE'RE THE BEST AT WHAT WE DO BECAUSE WE'VE SPENT OUR LIVES PROVING IT. AND, ONCE AGAIN, THE SAFETY OF THE ARKA RESTS ON OUR SHOULDERS, AND WE'RE GOING TO PUT A STOP TO ALL THIS NONSENSE, THE ONLY WAY THE WRITTEN KNOW HOW. I'M NOT ORDERING YOU TO GO, I'M SAYING LET'S GO DO OUR JOB, AND DO IT FUCKING WELL!

I'M SURE YOU ALL KNOW ME, AND FOR THOSE WHO DON'T THEN I EXPECT YOU SOON WILL. NO DOUBT YOU'VE HEARD ABOUT HELYARD, AND THE TRAITORS WHO KILLED THE SCHOLARS AT ARFELL. WORD HAS ALWAYS TRAVELLED FAST IN THESE PARTS.

I'M NOT GOING TO WASTE OUR PRECIOUS TIME TALKING, SO HERE'S THE PROBLEM. THE ONES WHO KILLED THE OLD SCHOLARS STOLE A BOOK, A POWERFUL SUMMONING MANUAL FROM THE TIMES OF THE DARK ELVES. USING THIS BOOK, THEY WANT TO RELEASE AN ANCIENT MONSTER THAT WILL TEAR EMANESKA INTO PIECES, AND NOW THAT HELYARD HAS BEEN THROWN IN JAIL, THE COUNCIL HAVE NO DOUBT THAT THE REST OF THESE TRAITORS WILL ACCELERATE THEIR PLAN.

A HUNDRED FISTS PUNCHED THE AIR TO HIS WORDS AND THE ROAR THAT ECHOED IN THE MARBLE HALL WAS FRIGHTENINGLY LOUD. FARDEN TURNED TO MODREN WITH A GRIN. HE INSTRUCTED HIM TO LEAD THE WRITTEN TO DUNYRA WHERE THEY WOULD MEET WITH THE DRAGONS. AND WITH THAT, FARDEN LEFT, HEADING OUT INTO THE EVENING, FOR THE CITY GATES AND BRIGHTSHOW.

IN THE DUNGEONS OF THE ARKETHEDRAL, JARRIK HAD BEEN ON WATCH FOR THE LAST TWELVE HOURS. . .
FIFTY THREE BRICKS. . .
FIFTY FOUR. . .
FIFTY FIVE. . .
GANLIR SHOULD BE HERE SOON.
HE'S PROBABLY FAST ASLEEP.
THE LAZY. . . ZZZ
A DARK SHADOWY FIGURE SLID INTO THE ROOM. . .
CREAK
TAKING KEYS FROM THEIR HOOK. . .
STEALING THE LIGHT FROM THE TORCHES. . .
LEAVING ONLY DARKNESS.

THE FIGURE CREPT THROUGH THE SHADOWS. HE FOUND HIS WAY TO THE THICK STEEL DOOR.
WITH A SCRAPING HE INSERTED THE STRANGE SHAPES OF METAL INTO THEIR HOLES
THERE WAS A DULL THUD AS HE PRESSED HIS PALMS TO THE OAK, RELEASING THE MAGICK SEAL HOLDING THE DOOR. . .
AND LOCKED IT WITH A SPELL OF HIS OWN.
WHAT DO YOU WANT FROM ME NOW?
WHO ARE YOU?
THE FIGURE TOOK A STEP FORWARD.
I'M A FRIEND.

I HAVE COME TO SET YOU FREE, YOUR MAGE.
FRIENDS SEEM HARD TO COME BY THESE DAYS. WELL WHATEVER IT IS YOU WANT FROM ME, LET'S GO.
WITH A CONTEMPTUOUS SNORT, THE HOODED MAN DREW A LONG WICKED KNIFE FROM BENEATH HIS CLOAK, READY TO STRIKE LIKE A COBRA. . .
BUT THE ARKMAGE WAS WAITING FOR HIM.

THOUGHT YOU COULD GET RID OF ME QUIETLY, DID YOU?
THOUGHT YOU COULD COME IN AND MURDER THE OLD MAGE IN HIS SLEEP, HMM?
WHO ARE YOU? ANSWER ME!
VICE?
SINCE THE BEGINNING.

SINCE THE BEGINNING...
THE BEGINNING, YES. I HAVE BEEN PLANNING THIS SINCE BEFORE YOU WERE ARKMAGE, HELYARD, SINCE BEFORE THE WAR.
WH... WHY?
WHY WHAT? YOU WERE JUST A DIVERSION, HELYARD, A SIMPLE PARLOUR TRICK OF SLEIGHT OF HAND TO KEEP ALL EYES ON YOU WHILE I WENT ABOUT MY BUSINESS.
OUR ARMY WILL BE SEVERAL HUNDRED MILES SOUTH OF WHERE THEY NEED TO BE. YOU FOOL. YOU FORGET THAT WITH YOU GONE, I ALONE COMMAND OUR MEN, AND ONCE I'M FINISHED WITH THEM, THE ARKA AND THEIR NEW FRIENDS THE SIRENS WILL BE NOTHING MORE THAN A FORGOTTEN SONG ON THE LIPS OF NEW EMANESKA.
YOU'LL NEVER WIN, VICE, THAT CREATURE WILL BE THWARTED BY OUR ARMY.
THEY'RE NOT MY PEOPLE!
YOU'VE BETRAYED YOUR OWN PEOPLE... THE SO CALLED UNDERMAGE IS NOTHING MORE THAN TRAITOROUS SCUM AFTER ALL. MAY THE GODS CURSE YOU VICE.
THE SAD THING IS, OLD FRIEND....
LET THE GODS CURSE ALL THEY WANT.
JARRICK HAD SLEPT THROUGH THE COMMOTION FROM DOWN THE HALL. VICE LEFT WITHOUT A SOUND AND THE SOLDIER SLUMBERED ON, DREAMING OF NOTHING IN PARTICULAR.

SEVEN HUNDRED MILES AWAY, ABOVE THE FOREST OF DURN...
A WHITE AND GOLD DRAGON CRASHED TO THE LEAFY FLOOR OF A CLEARING, SENDING STONES AND EARTH FLYING IN ALL DIRECTIONS AND CRUSHING A SMALL SAPLING.
SORRY ABOUT THE LANDING, FARDEN, MY LEGS HAVE CRAMPED UP AFTER THAT FLIGHT.
AS FARDEN HOPPED DOWN FROM THE SADDLE, HE GOT HIS FOOT TRAPPED IN THE LEATHER STIRRUP AND FELL TO THE LEAFY GROUND AWKWARDLY.
ARE YOU ALRIGHT?
MY FACE FEELS LIKE IT'S FROZEN SOLID, BUT APART FROM THAT I'M GOOD!
FARDEN LISTENED TO THE SOUND OF HER WINGS FADING INTO THE DISTANCE AS HE DISAPPEARED INTO THE THICK FOREST.
I'D BETTER BE GOING. GOOD LUCK FARDEN. I'LL SEE YOU AT KILTYRIN LATER TONIGHT.
FARDEN! BY THE GODS, YOU ARE ALIVE!
A SHORT WHILE LATER, FARDEN EMERGED FROM THE SCRAPING BRANCHES AND TWIGS AND STEPPED ONTO THE NEAT LAWN IN FRONT OF THE ARKABBEY.
WHEN HE REACHED DURNUS' ROOM THERE WAS LIGHT CREEPING OUT FROM UNDER HIS DOOR, SO FARDEN KNOCKED LOUDLY ON THE OAK AND WAITED.

YOU MUST EXCUSE ME, FARDEN, YOU CAUGHT ME IN THE MIDDLE OF MY EVENING MEAL.
AS ALWAYS, NO, BUT YOU CAN REST ASSURED THAT BOTHERSOME DUKE IN LEATH WILL BE MOST CONFUSED AS TO WHERE HIS BUTLER HAS DISAPPEARED TO.
THE SUBJECT OF DURNUS' DINNER HAD ALWAYS MADE FARDEN SLIGHTLY UNCOMFORTABLE. BUT THERE WERE OTHER THINGS ON HIS MIND.
THERE IS MUCH TO DISCUSS, OLD FRIEND AND WE DON'T HAVE MUCH TIME AT ALL.
I JUST RECEIVED WORD FROM A HAWK THAT HELYARD HAS BEEN THROWN INTO PRISON FOR TREASON. TELL ME THIS IS SOME SORT OF SICK JOKE.
ANYONE I KNOW?
SADLY I CAN'T, AND IT LOOKS AS THOUGH WE NEED YOUR EXPERTISE, OLD FRIEND.
FARDEN TOLD DURNUS OF NELSKA, AND THE PLOT TO USE AN OLD ELF WELL TO RAISE A MONSTER FROM THE OTHER SIDE. MAPS OF KILTYRIN WERE FETCHED FROM THE SHELVES, AND SOON ENOUGH DURNUS WAS PREPARING THE QUICKDOOR.
FARDEN LEFT AND HEADED FOR HIS ROOM FOR A QUICK LIE DOWN. HE STOPPED BY THE KITCHENS ON HIS WAY TO PICK UP A SNACK OR TWO.
HIS ROOM SEEMED COLD AND BARE COMPARED TO THE COSY ATMOSPHERE OF THE BEARDED GOAT BUT IT FELT GOOD TO BE BACK IN FAMILIAR SURROUNDINGS AGAIN.
THE ROOM WAS DARK SO HE REACHED FOR THE CANDLESTICK THAT SAT ON THE BEDSIDE TABLE. AS HE TRIED TO CLICK HIS FINGERS HE KNOCKED IT CLUMSILY AND IT FELL TO THE FLOOR WITH A DULL CLUNK.
LET IT GO SAID A VOICE. THE VOICE FROM HIS DREAMS.
A SMALL BARK-CLOTH BUNDLE CAUGHT HIS EYE, AND HE FROZE. LYING ON THE FLOOR WAS THE BUNDLE OF NEVERMAR. THE HAZY MEMORY OF HIDING IT INSIDE THE HOLLOW CANDLESTICK SUDDENLY CAME BACK TO HIM. HE GROUND HIS TEETH TOGETHER AND FELT TEMPTATION PRODDING HIM WITH A STICK AS IT ALWAYS DID.

WITH A GRUNT, THE MAGE STOOD UP AND LEFT HIS ROOM. HE RAN QUICKLY AND QUIETLY DOWN THE STAIRS UNTIL HE REACHED THE GROUND FLOOR AND THEN HE MADE FOR THE DOOR, STILL GRIPPING THE BUNDLE TIGHTLY IN HIS HAND.
HOOT
THE ONLY SOUNDS WERE THE WHISPERING BOUGHS SHAKING THEIR LEAFLESS BRANCHES AND THE SCREECHING OF THE DISTANT OWL. FARDEN LEANT UP AGAINST A TREE TRUNK.
AFTER MUCH DELIBERATING, FARDEN BIT HIS LIP, AND THE DRUG WON THE ARGUMENT. WITH A GRUNT, THE MAGE LIFTED THE LITTLE BUNDLE TO HIS NOSE AND SMELLED THE EARTHY, SICKLY-SWEET SCENT OF THE NEVERMAR.
WHAT ARE YOU DOING?
FARDEN IT'S ME!
ELESSI? WHAT ARE YOU DOING OUT HERE?
I COULD ASK YOU THE SAME QUESTION.
TELL ME THIS ISN'T YOURS, FARDEN, PLEASE.
I WAS GETTING RID OF IT, ELESSI. JUST GIVE IT TO ME.
NO. . .NO I WON'T.
THE MAID STUMBLED BACKWARDS AND TURNED TO RUN INTO THE FOREST BUT FARDEN GRABBED HER ARM BEFORE SHE COULD GET ANY FURTHER.

I WON'T HURT YOU, ELESSI BUT YOU NEED TO LISTEN TO ME! DURNUS MUST NOT KNOW ABOUT THIS, UNDERSTAND? I CAN'T LET HIM FIND OUT.
YOU'D BEST BE BEING HONEST WITH ME, FARDEN. YOU HEAR?
I CAME OUT HERE TO BURN IT, I SWEAR TO YOU. I'M FINISHED WITH IT... PLEASE.
FARDEN LIED.
IS THAT ALL YOU CARE ABOUT? WHAT ABOUT ME? THEY WILL HANG YOU FOR THIS. AND YOU, OF ALL PEOPLE.
THANK YOU.
PHIWP!
ALL OF A SUDDEN, THE METALLIC WHISPER OF SWORDS FLOATED ON THE BREEZE TO FARDEN'S KEEN EARS.
A BURST OF WHITE LIGHT BURNT AN ARROW TO CINDERS IN MID AIR.
I SUPPOSE THAT'S THE FIRST STEP THEN.
THERE WAS A BURST OF ORANGE LIGHT FROM BEHIND HIS FINGERS AND SMOKE CURLED AROUND HIS HANDS LIKE GREY LIQUID..
MOVE ELESSI! GO!
THE FOREST SUDDENLY CAME ALIVE WITH SHOUTS AND CRIES. DARK MEN WITH HIDDEN FACES SWARMED THROUGH THE TREES TOWARDS THEM, WAVING BLACKENED SWORDS AND CURVED KNIVES.

HALF AN HOUR LATER ...
WE JUST WANT TO TALK, OLD MAN, LET US IN!
WHAT ARE WE GOING TO DO?
CALM DOWN, WOMAN. FARDEN WILL BE HERE SOON. AND THEN WE CAN LEAVE!
I AM NO MAN!
UP IN THE FAR REACHES OF THE ABBEY TOWER, DURNUS PRESSED HIMSELF AGAINST THE DOOR AS THE MEN OUTSIDE CHARGED FOR THE TENTH TIME.
HE WAS A BLUR OF ANIMAL RAGE.
SO BE IT!
DURNUS FELT STRENGTH AND SPEED HE HADN'T KNOWN IN YEARS FLOWING THROUGH HIS DUSTY VEINS.
FARDEN WAS SUDDENLY AMONGST THEM,
HE SANK HIS FANGS INTO ANYTHING THAT MOVED.
FARDEN!
A MASKED ASSAILANT WAS LOCKED IN SLOW BATTLE WITH THE OLD VAMPYRE THE BLACKENED STEEL TIP BEGAN TO TICKLE THE PAPERY SKIN OF HIS NECK.

BOOT!!!
FARDEN, LET'S GET OUT OF HERE WHILE WE STILL CAN! COME ON!
I'M RIGHT BEHIND YOU!
ELESSI, I SWEAR TO THE GODS, I WILL CARRY YOU THROUGH THAT DOOR MYSELF IF YOU DON'T HURRY UP. IT'S NOT GOING TO BE OPEN MUCH LONGER!
GET YOURSELF THROUGH THE QUICKDOOR, ELESSI. NOW.
FARDEN! CAN WE GO NOW?!
FARDEN, YOU'RE BLEEDING!
DOES IT HURT?
WAS THAT A BIT MUCH?
YOU'LL FIND OUT ON THE OTHER SIDE.
NOT AS MUCH AS IT WILL IF YOU DON'T MOVE THAT BACKSIDE OF YOURS AND GET THROUGH THAT DOOR!
GO! BEFORE IT'S TOO LATE! I'LL FIGHT THE REST OFF.
FARDEN! THERE'S NO SHAME IN RUNNING TO FIGHT ANOTHER DAY!
THE VAMPYRE COULD ONLY NOD. HE UNDERSTOOD THE SITUATION. HE KNEW WHAT HAD TO BE DONE. MOUTHING A SWIFT GOOD LUCK, HE TURNED AND DISAPPEARED WITH A FLASH. THE ARCHES SHOOK AND WITH A GURGLING WHINE THE PORTAL VANISHED.
IT'S PERSONAL NOW.
THE SOUNDS OF METAL AND BOOTS GREW LOUD IN THE BLOOD-SPATTERED CORRIDOR. FARDEN GRIT HIS TEETH... HE RELISHED A GOOD FIGHT. IT WAS TIME TO MAKE THESE BASTARDS PAY.

"Beware the monster behind the door,
Watch for spiders all over the floor.
Be brave like your father, proud warrior and all,
Something is gnawing at bones in the hall.
Maybe you'll run, or maybe you'll fight,
Or maybe you'll sleep soundly all through the night.
Never you mind, now close your eyes,
Prey you sleep well, not be food for the flies."

~ Skölgard nursery rhyme ~

SOMEONE WAS SCREAMING IN THE LOCKED ROOM AT THE TOP OF THE SPIRE. THE CRIES OF PAIN WERE CHILLING, ACCOMPANIED BY THE HOWLING WIND THAT PAWED AT THE WINDOWS AND BATTLEMENTS OF THE TOWER.
THE ANCIENT-LOOKING SCRIBE HUMMED IN A DEEP DRONE AS HE WORKED, SINGING FORGOTTEN TUNES AND SONGS OF MAGICK TO HELP THE INK SETTLE AROUND THE NEEDLE'S POINT.
CHESKA SAT ON A LITTLE STOOL, SHAKING. TEARS ROLLED DOWN HER FACE AND DRIPPED ONTO A FLOOR THAT WAS ALREADY SOAKING WET FROM TWO DAYS' WORTH OF CRYING.
CHESKA WILLED HERSELF TO FEEL THE COLD BREEZE OF THE SHORE NEAR HER FATHER'S PALACE, THE SMELL OF THE PINES BY THE LAKE, THE SOUND OF THE WATERFALLS ROARING PAST HER WINDOW, BUT THE NEEDLE KEPT DRAGGING HER BACK TO THE TINY ROOM.
BRIM WAS TREMBLING. HE WISHED HE COULD PUT HIS HANDS TO HIS EARS AND BLOCK THE SOUNDS OF HIS FRIEND CRYING AND SCREAMING.
OUTSIDE THE SCRIBE'S ROOM, IN THE FIRST CHAMBER, BRIM SAT ON A LOW WOODEN BENCH BETWEEN TWO SERVANTS.
MAY I HAVE SOME WATER, BEFORE I GO IN...?
SCREAM!
SCR
EAM

A HEAVY BANG ECHOED FROM OUTSIDE THE CHAMBER, BACK ON THE STAIRS. THE TWO OLD MEN SWAPPED CONCERNED GLANCES.
THE SCRIBE HAD FINALLY STOPPED HUMMING. HE WIPED HIS NEEDLE CLEAN AND PLACED IT ON HIS LAP.
BRIM CRIED OUT AS THE DOOR SUDDENLY BURST INTO A THOUSAND FRAGMENTS.
THERE WAS A MOMENT OF UNEASY SILENCE BEFORE A MAN IN FULL CEREMONIAL ARMOUR FLEW THROUGH THE SMOKING DOOR FRAME AND CRASHED TO THE STONE FLOOR.
THE TWO OLD SERVANTS NEVER HAD A CHANCE.
A TALL FIGURE APPEARED THROUGH THE HAZE IN THE DOORWAY.
ANY PROFOUND WORDS IN YOUR LAST MOMENTS, MAGE?
...

CHESKA'S HEAD SWAM. SHE WATCHED THE SCRIBE FROM THE CORNER OF HER EYE. HE WAS RUSHING AROUND THE ROOM, BLOWING OUT THE CANDLES.
THERE WAS A HUGE CRASH AND THE SCRIBE SPUN AROUND TO SEE THE DOOR FLY INWARD UNDER A SHOWER OF SPARKS. A MAN STRODE THROUGH THE SPLINTERED DOORWAY AND STOOD IN THE DIM CANDLELIGHT.
I TAKE IT ALL IS IN ORDER?
YOU HAVE SERVED US WELL, SCRIBE.
HMM, YES, JUST AS YOU REQUIRED. SHE IS A STRONG ONE, FOR SURE..
THAT SOUNDS LIKE A GOODBYE, TO ME, VICE.
IT'S A SHAME THAT YOU HAVE WORN OUT YOUR USEFULNESS...
THE SONS OF ORION WILL GET WHAT IS COMING TO THEM IN THE END.
CHESKA TRIED TO MELT INTO THE SHADOWS OF HER HIDING PLACE, BUT SHE ALREADY KNEW WHAT WAS COMING. WHEN SHE OPENED HER EYES AGAIN THE FIGURE WAS STANDING OVER HER. HE LOOKED DOWN AND SMILED AT HER WICKEDLY. HE BRANDISHED A DRIPPING KNIFE IN HIS HANDS.
I TAKE NO PLEASURE IN DOING THIS,
THAT YOU HAVE.
YOU CAN'T FOOL ME MAGE, I HAVE SPENT A THOUSAND YEARS LISTENING TO YOU LIE.

BACK IN ALBION ...
HALF A DOZEN SERVANTS SAT KNEELING AROUND THE STATUE OF EVERNIA IN THE MAIN HALL OF THE ARKABBEY, COWERING AND FRIGHTENED. A SCORE OF MEN STOOD AROUND THEM HOLDING BLADES AND EYING THE SHADOWS.
WHERE IS FARDEN?
CONTROL YOURSELF. THERE'LL BE TIME FOR THAT LATER.
JUS' TELL US WHERE 'E IS AN' WE WON'T AF TO 'URT YOU, WILL WE MY PRETTY?
I... I TOLD YOU I DON'T KNOW, HE COMES AND GOES, WE NEVER SEE HIM!
NO? I THOUGHT NOT.
IF I DON'T START HEARING THE ANSWERS I WANT TO HEAR, PEOPLE ARE GOING TO START DYING ALL OVER AGAIN, UNDERSTAND?
MY MEN ARE GETTIN' RESTLESS.
I CAN ALWAYS LEAVE YOU AND YOUR MEN TO EXPLAIN TO MY EMPLOYER WHY YOU CAME BACK WITHOUT FARDEN'S HEAD IN A BAG...
IN THE DIM CANDLELIGHT, FARDEN COULD SEE THE BLACK SCRIPT ETCHED INTO THE PALE SKIN, ARKA BORN AND BRED, THAT MADE HIS BLOOD BOIL.
CURSE THOSE ALBION REPROBATES.
AFTER 'IM!.
GIVE HIM A HANDFUL OF MAGES AND THIS FARDEN WOULD HAVE BEEN TRUSSED UP AND STUFFED LIKE A BOAR BY NOW, IF ONLY HE...
FARDEN DASHED OUT OF THE DIM HALL, LEADING THE HOODED ATTACKERS AWAY FROM THE PRISONERS AND OUT INTO THE COLD NIGHT.

A DAY LATER. . .

NOTHING LIVED ON THE DUNWOLD MOORS. NOTHING. IF ONE WERE TO FIND THEMSELVES STANDING ON THE ROLLING HILLS AND DOWNS OF ALBION'S EASTERN COAST THEY WOULD FIND NOTHING BUT ROCKS AND WET GRASS WITH NO LIVING THING TO ACCOMPANY THEM.

FARDEN'S TIRED EYES ROVED OVER HIS SURROUNDINGS. HIS FOLLOWERS WERE NOWHERE TO BE SEEN, BUT HE KNEW THEY WEREN'T FAR BEHIND.

NEXT TO HIM A LITTLE POOL OF WATER HAD BEEN TRAPPED IN THE ROCK, SO HE BENT DOWN TO LOOK AT HIS HAGGARD REFLECTION. RED EYES AND THICK STUBBLE GREETED HIM LIKE THOSE OF A STRANGER.

HE LOOKED DOWN AT THE THICK ARROWSHAFT STICKING OUT OF HIS RIBS. HIS FINGERS WRAPPED TIGHTLY AROUND THE BLOOD-CAKED ARROWSHAFT AND YANKED. HARD. HE COULDN'T HELP BUT SCREAM. HIS PAIN ECHOED ACROSS THE MOORS.

THERE! COME ON LADS! 'E'S GOT NOWHERE T' HIDE NOW! I WANT 'IS HEAD ON A STICK!

FARDEN LURCHED INTO A WHEEZING RUN. THE WEIGHT. HE SUDDENLY REALISED. HELYARD'S WEIGHT. BUT THIS THING IN HIS HAND WAS DANGEROUS AND HE WOULD BE NO USE TO THE OTHERS DEAD.

BUT FARDEN HAD NO CHOICE, HE TRIED TO BEND ALL HIS BEING IN TO SEEING ONE PLACE. THERE WAS A DEAFENING CRACK AND THE AIR SPLIT IN TWO, DRAGGING HIM INTO THE DARKNESS AND INTO OBLIVION.

HUNDREDS OF MILES TO THE EAST, THE AIR CRACKED LIKE A WHIP AND SPLIT IN TWO LIKE A JAGGED GAP IN A WINDOW PANE.
THE MAGE STOOD AGHAST. HOT TEARS STUNG HIS EYES. AROUND HIM, WATER AND ICE MAGES BATTLED ON STUBBORNLY, HURLING SPELL AFTER SPELL AT THE INFERNO.
FARDEN HAD LANDED AT MANESMARK. HE FELT A SEARING HEAT ON HIS SKIN. ABOVE HIM, DRAGONS CIRCLED, HAULING BLOCKS OF ICE AND HUGE BARRELS OF WATER INTO THE SKY, DROPPING THEM ON TO THE BLACK, BURNING SKELETON OF THE SPIRE.
ER, THE... FIRE, SIR?
WHAT HAPPENED HERE?
FARFALLEN APPROACHED HIM.
IMAGES OF CHESKA TRAPPED IN A BURNING ROOM SPRANG UNBIDDEN INTO HIS HEAD, TAUNTING HIM CRUELLY WITH SICK REALITY.
HAVENHIGH, TELL US WHAT YOU FOUND.
GRAVE TIMES ARE UPON US, MAGE, AND IT IS WITH A HEAVY HEART THAT I GREET YOU.
THIS IS HAVENHIGH, ONE OF OUR YOUNGEST.
EARLIER THIS EVENING I SAW TWO BODIES PILED NEAR THE OTHER SIDE OF THE SPIRE. THEY WERE SCORCHED AND BURNT WITH SOMETHING MORE THAN JUST FIRE, THE HOLES IN THEIR BREASTPLATES TOLD ME AS MUCH. SOMEBODY STARTED THIS FIRE.
I THINK I KNOW SOMEONE THAT COULD TELL US WHAT HAPPENED HERE, IF WE ASKED HIM RIGHT.
THIS MAN WAS HIT BY A FIRE BOLT. THE OTHER THERE, SEE HOW THE HOLE IS LESS CHARRED AND SMALLER? THAT'S SPARK MAGICK.
WITHOUT A FURTHER WORD, THE MAGE WAS OFF, THE DRAGONS WATCHED HIM LEAVE AND FARFALLEN SIGHED QUIETLY TO HIMSELF.

THE GUARDS AT THE ARKATHEDRAL GATES WERE SILENT AND WARY OF FARDEN. WITH ANGRY EYES THEY LOOKED AT THE MAGE AS IF HE WERE SOMEONE TO BLAME, BUT THEY DID NOT CHALLENGE HIM, AND SO FARDEN LIMPED ON PAST.
STAIRS MADE HIS WOUND PROTEST AND SCREAM WITH FRESH AGONY, AND THE LONG HALLWAYS SEEMED ENDLESS. AS HE MADE HIS WAY DEEPER AND DEEPER INTO THE FORTRESS, THE WHITE MARBLE AND GOLD TRIMMINGS OF THE ARKATHEDRAL DISAPPEARED AND WERE GRADUALLY REPLACED BY DRAB GRANITE AND GLOOM.
NOBODY'S TO GO IN THERE, LORD VICE'S ORDERS, UNDER PAIN OF DEATH!
I DON'T HAVE TIME FOR THIS! NOW WHERE'S HELYARD?
FARDEN FOUND THE CELL DOOR AND GRITTED HIS TEETH,, THE SYMBOLS ON HIS WRIST BURNT WHITE LIKE FIRE UNDER HIS VAMBRACES. THE MAGE HAD NO TIME FOR SUBTLETY.
WITHOUT A SOUND, FARDEN STOOD UP AND WALKED OUT, LEAVING HELYARD IN PEACE. HE THOUGHT ONLY OF CHESKA.
HE BURST THROUGH THE HAZE AND STORMED INTO THE ROOM, FISTS CLENCHED AND FIRE TRAILING AROUND HIS WRISTS.
THE MAGE GINGERLY LIFTED HELYARD'S CHIN AND MOVED HIS HEAD SLIGHTLY, TRYING TO RESTORE SOME SENSE OF DECORUM TO THE OLD MAN'S POSTURE. WITH A GENTLE HAND HE CLOSED HIS EYES FOR THE FINAL TIME.

THAT EVENING THE CITY WAS FILLED WITH LIGHTS. ONE BY ONE, PEOPLE LEFT THEIR HOUSES CARRYING CANDLES IN GLASS JARS, OR TALL BLAZING TORCHES.
SILENT AND SOMBRE AND ALL TOGETHER THEY QUIETLY PROCEEDED DOWN TOWARDS THE SHORE. AN ARKMAGE HAD DIED.
THE BEARDED GOAT WAS QUIET FOR ONCE, SUBDUED AND HALF-EMPTY.
A SUDDEN, STRANGE EXCITEMENT STIRRED IN FARDEN'S CHEST.
THE MAGE SIPPED HIS SPICED WINE, SAVOURING THE STEAM ON HIS FACE. HE CAUGHT A FAMILIAR PAIR OF RODENT-LIKE EYES WATCHING HIM.
WHAT BRINGS YEW T' MY TABLE TONIGHT THEN?
HALF AN HOUR LATER, FARDEN FOUND HIMSELF IN THE BEGGAR'S ROOM.
LIGHT THE FIRE WOULD YEW BOY?
FARDEN BIT HIS TONGUE AND WENT TO THE FIREPLACE. HE CROUCHED LOW AND HUNCHED OVER SO THE MAN COULDN'T GET THE GRATIFICATION OF WATCHING THE SPELL.
ARE YEW GOIN' T' SMOKE IT OR KISS IT MAGE?
WHATS THAT?
NOTHING.
APPARENTLY NOT.
NOT DEAD YET THEN I SEE?
FARDEN LOOKED DOWN, CONFUSED, AND SAW A DIM GLOW COMING FROM HIS POCKET. IT WAS THE DAEMONSTONE HE HAD BOUGHT FOR CHESKA.

SMOKE IT!
FINE, I THINK IT'S TIME I LEFT.
FARDEN!
THE MAN SEEMED TO STRETCH BEFORE FARDEN'S EYES. HIS SKIN SHIMMERED AND WARPED.
YOU?
FARDEN ROARED, ALL WORDS FORGOTTEN, JUST PURE ANGER AND VENGEANCE POURING FROM HIS THROAT.
RAGE BEGAN TO BOIL IN THE MAGE'S HEART AND HE COULD FEEL THE WHITE HEAT ALONG HIS SPINE AND SHOULDERS.
THAT'S WHAT HELYARD SAID. YOU SHOULD THINK YOURSELF LUCKY I DIDN'T COME WHILE YOU WERE SLEEPING
THE ARROW WOUND BETWEEN HIS RIBS BURNT WITH AGONY. HE LOOKED UP TO FIND THE UNDERMAGE TOWERING OVER HIM.
FARDEN POUNCED, BUT VICE WAS READY FOR HIM. HE DROPPED TO HIS KNEES ND JABBED THE AIR. FARDEN COLLAPSED, DOUBLING UP WITH SEARING PAIN AND A YELL.
FARDEN SEIZED HIS NARROW OPPORTUNITY, BRINGING HIS KNEE STRAIGHT UP INTO VICE'S RIBS.

TASTE OF YOUR OWN MEDICINE, VICE? LIKE THE SCHOLARS AT ARFELL?
VICE THREW AN ELBOW IN FARDEN'S FACE, FORCING THE MAGE TO BREAK HIS HOLD AND STUMBLE BACKWARDS.
YOU ARE NO DIFFERENT FROM YOUR UNCLE FARDEN. THE TEMPER, THE NEVERMAR, THE VOICES IN YOUR HEAD, A LOST CAUSE.
VICE LAUGHED, AND A CURVED KNIFE APPEARED IN HIS HANDS, GLINTING EVILLY IN THE FIRELIGHT.
AND WHAT ABOUT THAT PRETTY GIRL IN THE SPIRE? SHE WAS SO EASY TO GET RID OF, AFTER ALL THE CONFUSION OF THE RITUAL. THE FIRE FINISHED HER OFF FOR ME, WHAT WAS SHE CALLED AGAIN?
DONT YOU FUCKING DARE SPEAK HER NAME!
FARDEN'S EYES BURNED WITH A VENGEFUL FIRE. THEY WERE FIXED ON THE UNDERMAGE, AND HE SHOOK AS THE MAGICK RUSHED THROUGH HIS VEINS, AS THOUGH HIS BLOOD BOILED.
VICE BEGAN TO BACK AWAY CAUTIOUSLY, A DIFFERENT EXPRESSION NOW ON HIS FACE.
THEN A ROAR CAME, A DEAFENING, EAR-SPLITTING ROAR FROM BELOW THEM THAT DROWNED OUT THE WORLD. THE FLOOR BETWEEN THEM BURST INTO A THOUSAND PIECES, AS IF A VOLCANO HAD SUDDENLY ERUPTED IN THE BAR.

WITH AN EXPLOSION OF SEARING FLAME, A WHITE- HOT PILLAR OF FIRE THROUGH THE ROOM AND INTO THE CEILING.
BOTH MEN FLEW BACKARDS, TRYING DESPERATELY TO ESCAPE THE FLAMES.
THE UNDERMAGE SCRAMBLED ONTO THE WINDOWSILL AND DISAPPEARED INTO THE SNOW-STREAKED SKY.
FARDEN SKIRTED THE FLAMES AND DASHED TO THE WINDOW. THE MAGE SCANNED THE GAWKING FACES BELOW HIM AND SPIED A FIGURE HURRYING THROUGH THE CROWD, HOOD UP AND ESCAPING.
WITH A SNARL, FARDEN LEAPT FROM THE BLAZING ROOM AND DOWN INTO THE BUSTLING, SCREAMING STREET BELOW. SNOW FLEW FROM HIS HEELS AS HE GAVE CHASE.
SEE YOU AT CARN BREAGH,
HE FOUND VICE IN THE NEXT STREET, WAITING AND GRINNING. BEFORE FARDEN COULD STOP HIM, THE UNDERMAGE GRABBED SOMETHING FROM INSIDE HIS CLOAK. THERE WAS A FLASH OF BRIGHT GOLD AND VICE VANISHED WITH A WHIP- CRACK, LEAVING THE AIR TO SHIVER BEHIND HIM.

FARDEN SLIPPED AND FELL TO THE COLD GROUND AND STARED IN HORROR AT THE EMPTY AIR.
NO NO NO!
THE SOUND OF WINGS BEATING THE AIR GREW LOUD.
FARDEN.
SEVERAL LOUD THUDS ECHOED ALONG THE STREET. THE COBBLESTONES SHOOK UNDER HIS KNEES. HE HEARD THE SCRAPING OF SCALES AND CLAWS ON STONE.
BEHIND THE MAGE STOOD FARFALLEN, AND THE BIG RED, TOWERDAWN. SVARTA WAS WITH THEM.
IT'S NOT LIKE I PLAN THESE THINGS.
WHAT HAPPENED HERE?
IT SEEMS THAT WHEREVER WE FIND DESTRUCTION AND CHAOS, WE FIND YOU.
HE'S GONE?
IT WAS VICE, IT'S BEEN HIM THIS WHOLE TIME! HE ESCAPED USING A WEIGHT, PROBABLY ÁDDREN'S
I SWEAR TO THE GODS, SVARTA, ONE MORE...
BOTH OF YOU BACK DOWN! HOW DOES THIS HELP US?
YOU LET HIM GO?!

I'LL ASK YOU AGAIN, WHERE IS THIS FOUL WORM?
THERE IS NO ELF WELL IN KILTYRIN, OR FIDLARIG. WE WERE CONNED! THE ARKA ARMY AND THE WRITTEN ARE HUNDREDS OF MILES FROM WHERE THEY NEED TO BE! VICE IS RELEASING HIS MONSTER AT CARN BREAGH. IT'S AN OLD FORTRESS TWO DAYS' MARCH FROM LEATH, EMPTY AND DEAD, OR AT LEAST WE THOUGHT. GODS DAMN IT!
WE HAVE TO STOP HIM.
THE MAGE IS RIGHT. WE HAVE NO CHOICE. VICE MUST BE STOPPED AT ALL COSTS. AND EVEN IF IT TAKES OUR LIVES, WE HAVE TO END THIS.
CARN BREAGH IN ALBION, NORTH OF LEATH. IT SEEMS THE BASTARD HAS DECEIVED US ONCE AGAIN
WE ARE NOT SERIOUSLY CONSIDERING THIS...
TOWERDAWN, ASSEMBLE ALL OUR FORCES IMMEDIATELY. SEND TWO OF OUR FASTEST, HAVENHIGH AND ANOTHER, ONE TO NELSKA AND ONE TO THE REST OF THE DRAGONS IN KILTYRIN. WE WILL NEED ALL THE HELP WE CAN GET.
FARDEN, YOU CAN RIDE WITH BRIGHTSHOW. HER RIDER IS IN ALBION WITH YOUR MAGES.
MAY THE GODS FLY ALONGSIDE US TONIGHT.
IT'S ORGANISED SUICIDE, EVEN WITH ALL OUR DRAGONS.
WITHIN HALF AN HOUR, FARFALLEN'S DRAGONS WERE TEARING THROUGH THE SNOWY SKIES. THEIR WINGS POUNDED THE TURBULENT AIR, PUSHING THEM THROUGH THE THICK STORMS OF THE MOUNTAINS UNTIL THEY SOARED ON THE CRISP AIR BETWEEN THE CLOUDS AND THE STARS. THE BRIGHT MOON SHIMMERED ACROSS THEIR SCALES.
FARDEN PULLED HIMSELF AS CLOSE TO BRIGHTSHOW AS HE COULD, USING HIS SPELLS TO KEEP HIMSELF WARM. IT WAS HARD TO BREATHE THE RUSHING AIR, AND EVERY TIME HE LOOKED DOWN HE FELT DESPERATELY SICK. HE JUST SHUT HIS EYES AND SIMMERED WITH HIS MAGICK, READY FOR BATTLE.

STATUE INSCRIPTION:
"WHEN THE SONS OF GODS WENT TO THE DAUGHTERS OF MAN AND HAD CHILDREN BY THEIR WOMBS, THEY BECAME THE GIANTS OF OLD, THE NEFALIM, "MEN" OF RENOWN AND INFAMY, DANGEROUS LIKE WOLVES AMONGST SHEEP."
FROM THE 'GATHERED PROPHETICS'
DAWN WAS SLOWLY BREAKING OVER ALBION. CARN BREACH SQUATTED QUIETLY ON ITS GREY-WHITE HILL, UNASSUMING AND PEACEFUL.
FAR BENEATH THE DRIPPING STONE, UNDER THE SOLID ROCK FLOORS, WHERE THE TORCHES STRUGGLED TO BURN THROUGH THE DARKNESS, VICE PORED OVER A SMALL DRAGONSCALE BOOK.
UNDERMAGE, THEY'RE HERE!
LET'S GIVE THEM A WELCOME THEY'LL NEVER FORGET.
HEAR ME.
A GUST OF WIND AROSE, SWIRLING THE ANCIENT DUST LIKE A STORM. STONE CHIPS AND SPLINTERS FLEW. CARN BREACH BEGAN TO SHAKE ITSELF IN TWO.
THE WHOLE ROOM LURCHED, CRACKLING WITH ENERGY. THE ELF WELL, THE GREAT BLACK ABYSS IN THE STONE FLOOR, BEGAN TO THRUM. IT SOUNDED AS THOUGH A HAMMER WAS STRIKING A DRUM IN ITS HELLISH DEPTHS.
AS VICE STRAINED TO READ THE SPELL ALOUD, HE DID NOT DARE TO TEAR HIS EYES FROM THE WELL. OUT OF THE DARKNESS BELOW, A HEAD ROSE UP; A MASSIVE, UGLY HEAD THAT WAS TOO HORRIFYING TO COMPREHEND.

HIGH IN THE ATMOSPHERE, WHERE THE AIR GREW THIN, A SWARM OF DRAGONS WHEELED AND CIRCLED ABOVE THE CRUMBLING FORT. ONE BY ONE, THEY FOLDED BACK THEIR WINGS AND PLUMMETED THROUGH THE AIR LIKE FALCONS.
THE AIR SCREAMED PAST HIS EARS LIKE BANSHEES. HIS INSIDES LURCHED UP AND DOWN AS THOUGH HIS STOMACH WAS BRAWLING WITH HIS LUNGS.
HOLD ON, FARDEN!
THE MAGE PRESSED HIMSELF AGAINST BRIGHTSHOW'S BACK AND TRIED DESPERATELY TO CLOSE HIS EYES, BUT SOMETHING INSIDE HIM COULDN'T TEAR ITSELF AWAY FROM THE TERRIFYING RIDE.
WE'RE TOO LATE!
IT'S A FUCKING HYDRA!
"GO AFTER VICE. CUT THE HEAD FROM THE SNAKE AND THE BODY DIES!" FARDEN HEARD A DEEP VOICE IN HIS HEAD, AS CLEAR AS IF SOMEONE SAT BEHIND HIM.
BRIGHTSHOW! TAKE ME DOWN TO THE CASTLE.
ARE YOU SURE?
MORE THAN EVER!
THE THING WAS TERRIFYING, IF ONLY BY SHEER SIZE. WITH A RUMBLE IT PULLED THE LAST OF ITS HEADS FROM THE RUIN AND STOOD TALL ON ALL FOUR MONSTROUS FEET,

BRIGHTSHOW DROPPED LIKE A STONE AND ROLLED, MAKING THE SNOW THE SKY AND BACK AGAIN. ABOVE THEM, FARDEN GLIMPSED DARK SHAPES FALLING WITH THEM, ROARING AND SCREECHING AND TRUMPETING. WHEN THE GROUND REARED UP, BRIGHTSHOW SKIMMED LOW. FARDEN LEAPT FROM HER SIDE AND DREW HIS SWORD. SNOW CRUNCHED UNDER HIS BOOTS.
GO, WHILE YOU STILL CAN!
JUST KEEP CLEAR OF THAT THING!
A BIG HAND GRABBED THE MAGE'S SHOULDER AND HE WHIRLED AROUND TO FIND EYRUM STANDING BEHIND HIM.
THEN LET US FINISH THIS, YOU AND I.
HAVE YOU STILL GOT THE SCALE I GAVE YOU?
FARDEN NODDED, THE FEELING OF THE SMALL TRINKET SUDDENLY COMFORTING HIM.
THE TWO RIPPED INTO THE STRONGHOLD, SMASHING DOORS FROM THEIR HINGES. EYRUM'S WINDMILLING AXE SLASHED AT ANYTHING THAT GOT IN HIS WAY. BLOOD FILLED THE AIR.
THE SOLDIERS KEPT COMING, POURING OUT OF HIDDEN DOORS AND SHADOWS LIKE RODENTS ON A SINKING SHIP.
FARDEN JUMPED FORWARDS AND SWUNG HIS LONGSWORD IN WILD ARCS. SOMETHING WHISPERED TO HIM INSIDE HIS HEAD. "WE'RE RUNNING OUT OF TIME."
AS HE FOUGHT, FARDEN SPIED A TALL FIGURE STANDING BACK FROM THE FIGHTING. THE MAGE SNARLED, AND THE RAGE STARTED TO BURN AFRESH IN HIS CHEST.

HIGH ABOVE THE RUINS OF CARN BREAGH, FARFALLEN WAS WATCHING HIS DRAGONS FALL LEFT AND RIGHT AND BY THE DOZEN.
WE CAN'T GO ON LIKE THIS, FARFALLEN! WE AREN'T EVEN HURTING IT!
EVERYONE ATTACK ONE HEAD AT A TIME! WE WILL NOT REST UNTIL THEY ALL LIE SMOKING IN THE RUINS. NOW FOLLOW ME!
THE DRAGONS ROARED TOGETHER AS THEY FOLLOWED THEIR LEADER, MOUTHS FULL OF SCORCHING FLAME. FARFALLEN LEAD THEM AGAINST THE LARGEST OF THE HYDRA'S HEADS. A STORM OF FIRE ENVELOPED IT, MAKING THE COLD AIR SNAP IN THE HEAT.
IT WORKED!
ONLY EIGHTEEN MORE TO GO, THOUGHT FARFALLEN. BUT HIS SMILE DIED ALL TOO QUICKLY. SOMETHING WAS HAPPENING TO THE DYING HEAD.
THE HEAD BUCKLED AS ITS NECK COLLAPSED BENEATH IT. LIKE A FALLING TREE IT TOPPLED OVER WITH AGONISING SLOWNESS, BUBBLING AND WAILING AS IT DIED.
IT WAS SPLITTING IN HALF. TWO HEADS ROSE UP IN ITS PLACE, GOOD AS NEW AND JUST AS DANGEROUS. THE HYDRA WHINED MOCKINGLY.

IN THE DEPTHS OF THE RUINED FORTRESS, FARDEN STEPPED INTO A FLICKERING SHAFT OF SUNLIGHT TO FACE HIS ENEMY.
YOU NEVER LEARN DO YOU, FARDEN? YOU NEVER STOP TO THINK.
I DON'T NEED TO THINK ABOUT KILLING YOU, IT'S THE OBVIOUS CHOICE.
HAH! AS IF YOU'VE EVER HAD A CHOICE.
I'VE BEEN PULLING YOUR STRINGS SINCE THE BEGINNING, FARDEN. THERE WERE TIMES I THOUGHT YOU WOULD BREAK, LIKE YOUR UNCLE. RUN NAKED THROUGH THE CITY STREETS. BUT YOU LASTED UNTIL THE END, AND YOU WERE VERY USEFUL INDEED. NOW, IT'S TIME TO GIVE IN AND DIE LIKE A GOOD BOY!
DID YOU REALLY THINK YOU COULD STOP ME?
ENOUGH TALK!
FARDEN LEAPT FORWARD AND STABBED AT HIM. BUT THE UNDERMAGE WAS FAST. A FLASH OF LIGHT FROM HIS HAND HIT THE SWORD AND THE BLADE BOUNCED AWAY WITH A LOUD CLANG.
VICE SHOCKED FARDEN WITH A SWIFT BOLT OF LIGHTNING, RIBBONS OF BLUE LIGHT DANCED ALL OVER HIS BODY AND SHOOK HIM WITH THEIR THUNDER.
HMM? ANSWER ME!
WHO DO YOU THINK YOU ARE, TO STAND IN MY WAY?
WITH ALL THE SPEED AND STRENGTH HE COULD MUSTER, FARDEN RAMMED HIS FOREHEAD INTO THE BRIDGE OF THE UNDERMAGE'S NOSE WITH A LOUD GRUNT.
AT THE SAME TIME HIS FINGERS CURLED INTO A FIST AND HE BROUGHT IT UP UNDER HIS CHIN.
VICE REELED BACKWARDS AND STAGGERED, JUST FOR A MOMENT.
EYRUM WAS SURROUNDED, WITH ONLY ONE SIREN STILL STANDING BY HIS SIDE
FARDEN, LIKE I SHOWED YOU!
FARDEN SPIED THE MANUAL SITTING ON A PEDESTAL.
VICE SAW THE LOOK IN HIS EYES AND CAST A BLISTERING FIREBALL AT THE MAGE AS HE STUMBLED. FARDEN TENSED, WILLING ALL HIS MAGICK FORWARD. WITH ONE TINY STEP, HE SLIPPED TO THE SIDE AND THE ROOM BLURRED LIKE A RUINED OIL PAINTING. HE FELT THE HEAT OF THE FIREBALL KISS THE BACK OF HIS NECK AS THE WORLD WAS WIPED ASIDE.

FARDEN SKIDDED TO A HALT AND GRABBED THE LITTLE BOOK. HE LET THE MAGICK FLOW INTO HIS HANDS AND ERUPT IN WHITE HOT FLAMES.
VICE LANDED A BLOW TO HIS RIBS RIGHT WHERE THE ARROW HAD HIT HIM. BLINDING PAIN KNOCKED HIM TO THE FLOOR.
A DULL BOOM ECHOED THOUGH THE DEPTHS OF THE WELL. THE ROOM STARTED TO SHAKE ANEW AS THE YELLOW PAGES OF THE BOOK CURLED AND CRUMBLED.
SOMETHING OR SOMEONE WAS STANDING BEHIND HIM, BUT AS HE TURNED, A HEAVY OBJECT COLLIDED WITH HIS SKULL, AND THE WORLD WENT BLACK.
WE HAVE TO FALL BACK, THE MAGE HAS FAILED.
I CAN STILL FEEL HIM, SOMEWHERE IN THERE.
FARFALLEN...
FARFALLEN LET A WAVE OF PAIN PASS OVER HIM, AND NODDED SLOWLY.
SOUND THE RETREAT! LET US GET AWAY FROM THIS THING! WE HAVE DONE OUR BEST, EMANESKA WILL HAVE TO FEND FOR ITSELF.
A MIGHTY CHEER ROSE UP FROM THE DIMINISHED RANKS OF THE DRAGONS.
WAIT! SOMETHING'S HAPPENING!
A HUGE BOOM RESONATED FROM SOMEWHERE INSIDE CARN BREACH. FARFALLEN SQUINTED AT THE MONSTER. THE HYDRA'S FLESH SMOULDERED LIKE BURNING PAPER.
IT CRIED OUT WITH ITS MINOR CHORD WAIL FOR ONE LAST TIME. THERE WAS A LOUD SUCKING NOISE AS THE AIR RUSHED INWARDS AND THE HYDRA SEEMED TO FOLD IN ON ITSELF WITH A LOW RUMBLE.
FARFALLEN HAD ONLY ONE THING ON HIS MIND: FARDEN, THE LITTLE SPARK THAT HAD DISAPPEARED IN HIS MIND SHORTLY BEFORE THE HYDRA HAD COLLAPSED.

FARDEN WAS CONCENTRATING ON STAYING CONSCIOUS. HE HADN'T FELT SO CLOSE TO SLIPPING AWAY SINCE THE SHIPWRECK.
EVERYTHING IN THE ROOM HAD BEEN TURNED SHADES OF RED, GREEN, YELLOW, AND BLUE. FARDEN BLINKED, HARD, BUT THE COLOURS DIDN'T GO AWAY.
I'LL TAKE THESE.
FARDEN WAS IN THE ARKATHEDRAL. HE WAS SOMEHOW BACK IN KRAUSLUNG, NOT ALBION. HE PONDERED HOW LONG HE COULD HAVE BEEN THERE, TIED TO THE CHAIR IN THAT EMPTY ROOM. TWO BLURRY FIGURES WALKED IN TO THE ROOM, A TALL ONE AND ANOTHER, FARDEN COULDN'T MAKE THEM OUT.
VICE REACHED INTO FARDEN'S POCKETS TO RETRIEVE THE WEIGHT AND THE DAEMONSTONE, AND SLIPPED THEM BOTH INTO A POCKET OF HIS OWN.
HAH, I FIND THAT VERY UNLIKELY. I MIGHT AS WELL TELL YOU THAT AT THIS VERY MOMENT THE GOOD KING BANE IS PERUSING THE NEWEST ADDITION TO HIS REALMS.
I KILLED YOUR HYDRA, IT'S OVER
YOU WERE JUST AN EXPERIMENT, FARDEN. A WEAPON, THEN A TOOL. COME NOW, IS IT STARTING TO MAKE SENSE? HAVE YOU REALISED WHO ELSE I HAVE KEPT UNDER MY WING?
IN THE END, THE ONLY THING I NEEDED FROM YOU WAS YOU.
AND FARDEN, THE SO-CALLED SAVIOUR OF THE PROUD ARKA, WILL BE CHARGED WITH TREASON AND SENT TO THE GALLOWS TO HANG FOR ALL TO SEE.
YOU'RE NOTHING BUT A COMMON THIEF.
FOOTSTEPS ECHOED ON THE STONE AS THE OTHER FIGURE WALKED FORWARD INTO THE KALEIDOSCOPE LIGHT. THE BREATH CAUGHT IN HIS THROAT. HIS HEART GREW COLD. EVERYTHING WITHIN HIM CRUMBLED. IT WAS CHESKA.
I WILL BE BACK FOR YOU MOMENTARILY. I HAVE A PRINCESS TO RETURN TO HER FATHER, AND A CITY TO CLAIM.
IT WAS FUN, FOR A WHILE, AND WE GOT WHAT WE NEEDED.
A LITTLE SPARK OF LIFE GROWS INSIDE CHESKA'S WOMB, A CHILD OF PURE POWER BORN FROM TWO WRITTEN. THERE IS A REASON THE OFFSPRING OF SUCH A UNION IS OUTLAWED, FARDEN, AND THAT REASON IS VERY SIMPLE. YOUR CHILD WILL BE THE FINEST MAGE EMANESKA HAS EVER SEEN, AND MY FINEST WEAPON.
WITHOUT ANOTHER WORD, THEY LEFT AND THE DOOR SLAMMED BEHIND THEM. FARDEN STARTED TO CONVULSE, YANKING AND STRAINING THE ROPES IN ALL DIRECTIONS. THE CHAIR AND THE KNOTS PROTESTED WITH SQUEAKS AND GROANS BUT STILL THEY DIDN'T BUDGE. FARDEN CLOSED HIS EYES AND WEPT.

I DON'T UNDERSTAND WHY YOU HAD TO TELL HIM ABOUT THE CHILD, HE'S ALREADY GOING TO HANG, WHY RUB IT IN?
ARE YOU TURNING SOFT ON ME, CHESKA? THE MAN HAS CAUSED US ENDLESS TROUBLE, HE DESERVES TO SUFFER.
JUST REMEMBER WHAT I TOLD YOU.
THE KING OF SKÖLGARD TURNED AROUND TO FACE THE NEWCOMERS. WHEN HE SAW CHESKA, KING BANE OPENED HIS MASSIVE ARMS WIDE,
VICE PASTED AN AFFABLE SMILE ON HIS FACE AND WALKED INTO THE BRIGHT SUNLIGHT OF THE GREAT HALL.
CHESKA, MY DAUGHTER, IT IS GOOD TO HAVE YOU BACK IN MY ARMS ONCE AGAIN.
I WAS JUST ABOUT TO EXPLAIN. THE TRAITOR BEHIND ALL OF THIS IS NONE OTHER THAN ONE OF OUR OWN WRITTEN, A MAGE THIS COUNCIL PUT A LOT OF FAITH IN.
HE IS NONE OTHER THAN FARDEN.
WHERE IS THE BASTARD WHO DARED TO ENDANGER THE FIRST PRINCESS OF SKÖLGARD?
YOU ALLOWED HIM TO ESCAPE, ARKMAGE ADDREN, AFTER WHAT HE DID IN MANESMARK? AFTER HE ALMOST KILLED MY DAUGHTER? YOU ARE NOT FIT TO RULE THESE PEOPLE. DRAG HIM FROM THE THRONE!
YOU ARE ALL WITNESSES TO THIS! FROM HENCEFORTH THE LANDS BELONGING TO THE ARKA WILL BE HELD AS A VASSAL OF THE SKOLGARD EMPIRE! MY SOLDIERS WILL REMAIN HERE TO KEEP ORDER AS YOUR NEW ARKMAGE SEES FIT. SINCE HE HAS SAVED THIS COUNCIL FROM BETRAYAL AND CHAOS MORE THAN ONCE, I AM APPOINTING LORD VICE AS THE HEAD OF THIS COUNCIL, TO RULE ALONE. MY WORD IS FINAL!
THE COUNCIL BEGAN TO CLAP AS VICE PUT HIS FOOT ON THE MARBLE STEPS. ONE BY ONE, HE MARCHED UP THEM, AND THEN TURNED TO TAKE HIS PLACE ON THE THRONE. HE LOOKED OVER THE GATHERED MEMBERS OF THE COUNCIL AND THEN TO BANE, WHO STARED CONFIDENTLY BACK AT HIM WITH WHAT COULD HAVE BEEN A SMILE.

FARDEN OPENED HIS EYES TO FIND THE SUN AND A BLACK CAT STARING AT HIM.
I TOLD YOU TO LEAVE ME ALONE.
YOU'RE NOT FINISHED YET.
I'M DONE. I GIVE UP. ALL I HAVE TO LOOK FORWARD TO IS THE ROPE AROUND MY NECK.
SO THIS IS IT? ALL THE HELP I'VE GIVEN YOU AND YOU JUST GIVE UP?
I WANT TO BE LEFT ALONE.
THEY FOUND ME NAKED AND SCREAMING, PAINTED IN SOMEONE ELSE'S BLOOD.
THEY FOUND ME SCRAPING WORDS INTO MY LEGS WITH SHARDS OF WINDOW GLASS.
THEY SENT ME OUT INTO THE WILDERNESS. THEY DIDN'T KILL ME, THEY LET ME GO, I DIDN'T FIGHT, I LEFT. I WAS LUCKY.
HE HAD CHANGED ME, HE HAD TRIED TO USE ME, BUT I FAILED. HE HAD FAILED. ARE YOU HIS TOOL, FARDEN? HIS WEAPON?
FARDEN SHOOK HIS HEAD IN THE DREAM. HE COULD FEEL THE SAND OF HIS DESERT DRAGGING HIM UNDER, AND THE WIND TEARING AT HIS SKIN. AT FIRST, HE LET THEM TAKE HIM, BUT THEN HE THOUGHT OF VICE GRINNING VICTORIOUSLY AT THE CROWDS. OF CHESKA AT HIS SIDE, SMILING ALSO. OF THE CHILD WITHIN HER. THEIR CHILD. THAT ALONE PULLED HIM BACK. NO, FARDEN TOLD HIMSELF. HE WOULD NOT BE HUNG AND FORGOTTEN. HE WOULD FIGHT.
ARE YOU HIS TOOL, FARDEN?!
NO I AM NOT.
THEN PROVE IT!
FARDEN SNAPPED BACK TO CONSCIOUSNESS AS THE STAINED GLASS BEHIND HIM SHATTERED INTO A THOUSAND PIECES. GOLD WINGS TOWERED OVER HIM. IT WAS FARFALLEN. THE DRAGON RAKED A RAZOR-SHARP TALON OVER THE BACK OF THE CHAIR AND FARDEN'S BONDS SPRANG OPEN WITH A TWANG.
I HAVE TO TRY! JUST KEEP THEM OFF MY BACK!
THE KING OF SKÖLGARD HAS TAKEN OVER THE CITY, YOU DON'T HAVE MUCH TIME TO STOP VICE!

FARDEN WAS CHASED BY SHOUTS AND THE CLANGING OF WEAPONS AS HE RAN, BLOODY FEET SKIDDING ON THE MARBLE FLOORS.
HALT!
FARDEN DID NO SUCH THING. HE FLUNG OUT HIS HANDS AND THE GUARDS FLEW BACK AGAINST THE DOORS OF THE GREAT HALL WITH A CRASH.
SLAM!!
THE GREAT HALL WAS DEATHLY QUIET. EVERY EYE WAS ON FARDEN AS HE STOOD PANTING IN THE DOORWAY, CAKED IN BLOOD.
YOU'RE A STUBBORN BASTARD, FARDEN, JUST LIKE YOUR UNCLE. I WILL HAVE YOU HANGED IMMEDIATELY!
HAVE YOU TOLD THEM WHAT YOU TOLD ME VICE? HAVE YOU TOLD THEM ABOUT THE FIRE? ABOUT HELYARD? TELL THE COUNCIL WHAT YOU REALLY ARE, OLD FRIEND.
AMID SHOUTS AND PANICKED YELLS, FARDEN SPRINTED FORWARD. HE JUMPED AND SOARED THROUGH THE AIR, FOCUSING ALL HIS ENERGY INTO ONE CRUCIAL SWING FOR VICE'S FACE. IT CONNECTED WITH AN EXPLOSION OF LIGHT, AND THE TWO MEN SPRAWLED ON THE MARBLE.
HELYARD'S WEIGHT. IT LAY IN THE SCALES OF THE EVERNIA STATUE. IT COULD BE OVER IN AN INSTANT. VICE, CHESKA, THE ARKA, THEY COULD ALL DISAPPEAR.
FARDEN SCRAMBLED FOR THE GOLD DISK. HE SNATCHED IT FROM THE STATUE AND BENT HIS ENTIRE WILL TO IT. HE WATCHED AS THE WORLD GROUND TO A HALT. HE IGNORED THE GUARDS POISED OVER HIM WITH SWORDS AND SPEARS. HE LOOKED ONLY AT CHESKA. SHE WASN'T THE SAME TO HIM ANY MORE. JUST A HOLLOW SHELL OF THE PERSON HE HAD LOVED. THE WORLD FOLDED IN ON ITSELF, AND HE WAS DRAGGED INTO THE BLINDING LIGHT, AWAY FROM THE CHAOS.

A FEW MONTHS LATER, A SMALL BOAT APPROACHED THE SNOWY SHORES OF NELSKA WITH THREE PASSENGERS SITTING ON ITS WET BENCHES.
WHAT'S WRONG? YOU'VE BEEN FIDGETING AROUND THE WHOLE TIME.
NOTHING IS WRONG, MAID, I AM MERELY TIRED AND NOT FOND OF THE SEA.
WELL, YOU'RE ABOUT TO MEET ONE, BUT THEY'RE AS DOCILE AS BIG CATS. IT'S THEIR QUEEN YOU HAVE TO LOOK OUT FOR.
YOU TOLD ME YOU LOVED THE SEA.
NOT IN SMALL BOATS, NOW LEAVE ME ALONE.
ARE THE DRAGONS DANGEROUS? I'VE NEVER SEEN A DRAGON.
WELL MET AND GOOD WISHES, FRIEND. ANY NEWS FROM KRAUSLUNG?
AFTER A FEW MINUTES OF ROWING, THEY REACHED THE SHORE. A PAIR OF SIREN SOLDIERS DRAGGED THE BOAT UP ABOVE THE TIDELINE WHERE THE OTHERS WERE WAITING FOR THEM.
NONE. THE LAST WE HEARD SHE WAS OUT OF THE CITY AND IN THE NORTH, WITH HER FATHER. VICE REMAINS IN THE ARKATHEDRAL FOR NOW.
FARDEN WALKED TO THE DRAGONS AND SMILED AT FARFALLEN. SVARTA AND EYRUM WERE ON HIS LEFT, TOWERDAWN, HAVENHIGH AND BRIGHTSHOW STOOD ON HIS RIGHT WITH THEIR RIDERS.
DARK TIMES ARE AHEAD; HE HAS NO LOVE FOR US DRAGONS.
YOU SHOULD HAVE KILLED VICE WHEN YOU HAD THE CHANCE.
IT IS A PLEASURE TO MEET YOU, ELESSI OF ALBION.
IN CASE YOU FORGOT, FARDEN, YOU LEFT SOMETHING BEHIND THE LAST TIME YOU WERE HERE.
I'VE HEARD A LOT ABOUT YOU, DURNUS, AND LET ME TELL YOU WHAT AN HONOUR IT IS TO MEET YOU. IT IS A PLEASURE TO HAVE YOU ALL IN NELSKA.
IT WAS LAZY, THE SHIP'S CAT. WHEN IT SAW DURNUS STANDING THERE IT WANDERED FORWARD PONDEROUSLY, DAINTILY STEPPING OVER THE WET PEBBLES.
IS THIS NORMAL IN NELSKA?
NOT IN THE SLIGHTEST.
I HAVE A MESSAGE FOR THE VAMPYRE.
SAID THE CAT.

the written

BY BEN GALLEY

ART BY MIKE SHIPLEY

KICKSTARTER

AND NOW TO THANK THE KICKSTARTER BACKERS, ALL 166 OF YOU! WITHOUT YOU, THIS GRAPHIC NOVEL WOULD NEVER HAVE EXISTED, LET ALONE PUBLISHED AND ENJOYED. MIKE AND MYSELF THANK YOU FOR YOUR SUPPORT AND YOUR PATIENCE WHILE WE'VE TOILED TO MAKE THIS NOVEL A REALITY. I HOPE YOU ENJOYED WHAT YOU HELPED CREATE, AND OF COURSE, ENJOY YOUR WELL-DESERVED REWARDS.

THANK YOU – BEN & MIKE

NOW ON TO THE MENTIONS:

THE FULL UNDERMAGE PACKAGE
THE EXCLUSIVE ARKMAGE HAMPER
THE DAEMON'S DANGLIES

FOR THOSE OF YOU WHO ARE KEEN OF EYE, YOU MIGHT HAVE SPOTTED SOME FAMILIAR FACES DOTTED HERE AND THERE THROUGHOUT THE NOVEL. THESE ARE THE BACKERS THAT MANAGED TO GET THEIR HANDS ON THE REWARDS ABOVE – THE CHANCE TO GET THEIR FACES DRAWN INTO THE ACTUAL ARTWORK!

ALEX DIAZ

ABBE ESTEVEZ

BRANDON HAUSAUER

DREW BRIDGER

ETIENNE BOUCHER STE-MARIE

HARRIET GEMMELL

JENNIFER COGAR

JORG ANCRATH

JON DOWLING

JASON BENNETT

KAREN HUXLEY

MARCUS BRUCKNER

MARCUS COSTELLO

MITCHELL TOBY JOHNSON

MR. & MRS. RACHID

NANCY CLARK

NEILL RAMSEY

NICK SUFFOLK

PATRICK S. CAHIWAT

REECE BRIDGER

STEPHEN MCMANUS

STEVEN HEWITSON

STEPHEN HASKINS

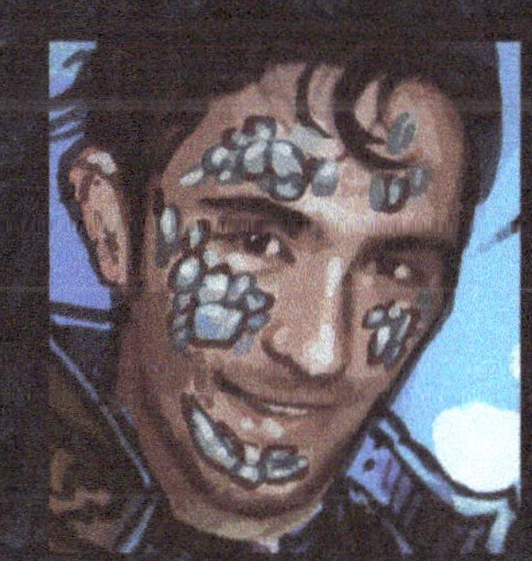

ROBERT LUNA

RONALD ADAMS

T.J. OLSON

AND THANK YOU ALSO TO NIX, PAUL GALLEY, TAN U-PENG, AND BRIAN OLSON

<h1 style="color:#e8542f">THE FARDEN SPECIAL
THE WRITTEN CLASSIC COMBO</h1>

AS WELL AS THE EXCLUSIVE BOTTLE
OPENERS, THESE BACKERS SNAGGED THE
FIRST PAPERBACK COPIES IN THE WORLD,
AND SIGNED COPIES TO BOOT!
THANK YOU VERY MUCH FOR YOUR
SUPPORT:

TO GET YOUR HANDS ON
THE REST OF THE
EMANESKA SERIES, VISIT
WWW.BENGALLEY.COM